ECLECTIC BREW

Edited by

Bette Hileman and Katherine Mercurio Gotthardt

Writing and art by members and friends of Bull Run
Unitarian Universalists, Manassas, Virginia

Published by
Bull Run Unitarian Universalists
9350 Main Street
Manassas, Virginia 20110
Phone: 703-361-6269
Web: www.bruu.org

The mission of the Bull Run Unitarian Universalists congregation is to nurture ourselves, our children, our community, and our natural world in the pursuit of spiritual and intellectual growth. We give expression to our mission through celebrating our diversity and giving of our talents and resources with justice, equity, and compassion.

Cover design by K Art and Design, Inc., Culpeper, Virginia.

Cover image by Lydia Bratton.

Text layout by Bette Hileman

Edited by Bette Hileman and Katherine Mercurio Gotthardt

ISBN 978-1456344917

Library of Congress Catalog Number: 2011900533

Printed in the United States of America

TABLE OF CONTENTS

PREFACE

The word "anthology" is associated with several images, the most popular being a collection of brief literary pieces inflicted on high school and college students. However, that requirement is quickly over, to the relief of those uncomfortable with poetry and fiction. Some of us may also have been exposed to anthologies released by publishers who offer practiced, new, or emerging artists more readership than they might have received had they published independently.

What most readers do not know is that the word anthology has historically meant "flower gathering." This definition comes from the Greek "*anthos*" meaning "a flower," "*logia*" meaning "collection or collecting," and "*legein*" meaning "gather." The modern use of the word, then, is metaphoric and apropos.

The literature and art gathered in this book are indeed representative of a garden—of ideas, genres, and images—seeded more than a year ago by the Bull Run Unitarian Universalists Writers' Group. From the hearts and minds of authors and artists both inside and outside, the group has blossomed with creativity offered freely and joyfully. The pieces are meant to inspire and encourage thought. We hope that at least some of what you will read and see in this book will achieve that end.

Katherine Mercurio Gotthardt, Editor and Writers' Group Facilitator

Bette Hileman, Editor

ACKNOWLEDGMENTS

It takes a team to put together an anthology like this, and we are so grateful for that team. Hence, appreciation goes out to the members and friends of Bull Run Unitarian Universalists congregation in Manassas, Virginia, who submitted quality writing, photographs, and drawings, as well as to the administrative staff, who made this project happen.

Many thanks also to members of the editorial board, particularly to Bette Hileman, who devoted more than one hundred hours editing and designing this book, and to Ron Kendrick, who during the final two weeks of editing created nine drawings for the book.

Editorial Board

Bette Hileman, Editor
Katherine Mercurio Gotthardt, Editor
Steve Clapp, Editorial Board Member
Richard Demaret, Editorial Board Member
Sheila School, Editorial Board Member
Duncan Shea, Editorial Board Member

FICTION

PUBLIC WELFARE

Katherine Mercurio Gotthardt

They don't call it "welfare" anymore. It's the Department of Transitional Assistance. But that doesn't make it better. The benches are still hard and worn, the smoothed wood glaring through remains of honey-colored stain. The floors are still tiled in Sixties charcoal-grey with white swirls. The walls are still ivory, smeared by the dirty fingers of a million children, and the lighting is still fluorescent, flickering in the windowless waiting room. And me. I am still there after three hours of waiting. A monument to the system. Still jobless. They keep telling me I will find something. But there is nothing out there for me.

How I came to be in the office is a long story, for which I will give only a synopsis. At eighteen, I divorced my husband, handed over my eight-month-old girl to him, and took off to start over, earn my fortune. I worked for Macy's. I was a cashier. Every day, banging figures into the register while these pretty women in ninety-dollar shoes frowned at my polyester dress and press-on nails. I just couldn't take it anymore. All those beautiful clothes that I could never buy, even with my discount.

I didn't know they had such good store security. I thought with a few dresses and a pair of nylons, I would be satisfied. I didn't think about how I'd actually wear the stuff and have to explain where I'd bought it.

A year later, I stood in front of a judge, the words "ten thousand dollars" screaming at me. I didn't have to do time. I did community service—for free. For two years. But I still had to pay off the debt. I still owe on it. I don't even have most of the clothes anymore. They made me give back the stuff that had tags on it. So I did. But I still have a criminal record.

There was this one dress I could not stand to give back. I love it so much. I remember a certain day at the welfare office because I was wearing this dress. It makes me feel special to wear it. It's navy blue with a sailor's collar and has a smart-looking red bow in front. The skirt is pleated and long, and it's made of some material that can only be dry-cleaned. I never have money for dry-cleaning, so I had to hand-wash the dress a few times. It has shrunk a little, but it's still okay.

I wore the dress with some off-white pantyhose and cheap patent-leather shoes I'd gotten at the Salvation Army thrift store. I can't believe some of the good stuff they have there. The shoes were almost new. I washed them with Ajax scrub in case they had fungus in them. They still shine even now. I was careful not to scrub the patent off.

My pantyhose had a little run in the ankle that day, and I didn't have any clear nail polish, so I used a drop of red from an almost empty bottle. But I was afraid it would show, so on top of that I put a little school glue just to make the patch white and reinforce the job I'd already done. I looked nice. Respectable. I like to look respectable when I go to the welfare office. I don't like the employees to think they are handing out charity to a freeloader.

I sat on the bench, waiting for them to call my number. I sat very still and straight with good posture, thinking. There is a man that comes in every time I am there. He is about my age, but his clothes are dated and he stoops. His hair is long and greasy and looks like it should be blond. He looks at least ten years older than me, but he's not that old. He slings this ripped army bag around his shoulders and slumps. His shirt always catches in the strap, and his hair, the few parts that aren't greasy, looks wild from the static the bag gives off. When I see him, I always think, "Thank God I don't look like that."

Some things always happen the same way when you come to this place, so I thought I would see him again that day. The place is so unchanging, sometimes I start to lose track of what day it is and how long I've been coming here. It's like my history keeps repeating itself. It's not a good history really.

I pressed my back against the wood and stared at the clock. It's one of those white-faced clocks with a black plastic frame, the kind you see in schools. I find if I focus on something, I don't look like I really belong in the office. I know because I practiced this in the room I rent. I look more removed, like I'm thinking some very important thoughts. If you think that much, you must not be a client. You must be a lawyer or a caseworker waiting for an interview or something. But you definitely don't belong here.

I play the clock game a lot. Of course, it doesn't work on people like the real caseworkers and the attendants and the man I always see here. They see me every month. So obviously I'm a client. But the others are complete strangers or they have dementia or they don't care or they just aren't very smart. So I know it works on them.

Gloria, the lady behind the window, has a face like a sunflower—round, gritty and yellow. Her curly, dyed hair reminds me of the petals. But she is not sunny at all. She doesn't smile, and I think she has said "please" only once since I've been coming—something like three years now. My time is almost up. They'll boot me out of the system, and then I don't know what I'll do. No one will hire me. I have a record.

The person Gloria said "please" to wasn't me. It was some mailman or delivery guy. He didn't come in that day, though, so there was no "please" to be heard out of her mouth. That day, Gloria wore a white, shiny shirt printed with huge teal and gold and red diamonds. Very ugly. But she never has to worry about style. She doesn't have to impress anyone. I don't think she's married, and I doubt she has a man. Who would want to go out with Gloria?

So there was Gloria behind her glass, with the little slot cut out at the bottom so she wouldn't get breathed on by the rest of us and could pass papers to us like we were prisoners and she wasn't. The greasy-haired man did come in around one o'clock. I still sat waiting for my number and for the hundredth time, just for something to do, tried to catch his name when he checked in. That's the weird thing. All this time and I've still never heard his name. He kind of mumbles, and every time, Gloria has to say, "You have to speak up, sir," in a voice that would make most people want to whisper instead of do what she says. She's just that kind of person.

Greasy Hair finished his business and sat down, right next to me. In fact, it was the first time it ever happened. Usually, he sits across the room. I crossed my legs and looked harder at the clock. If I'd had something to read, something smart-looking like a leather-bound novel or legal textbook, I would have taken it out to make myself seem more unapproachable. Instead, I had to sit there and cringe because this guy kept looking at me. I hoped he didn't want to start a conversation because I wasn't up to it. Not with him anyway.

More people walked in, and it sounded like a class of tenth graders was there. A line formed behind the counter, and I watched through the corner of my eye as people checked in with Gloria, got a number, and found a place to sit. When there were no more benches, people started sitting on the floor or leaning against the wall. "*Dios mio*, fucking line," a Latino woman said and not quietly.

"Yeah," said a white guy in overalls too short for him. He wasn't wearing socks with his sneakers. "Sucks today, don't it?"

"Sucks every day," a petite black lady said and gave a deep chuckle that made me wonder where in her little body that voice came from.

The good thing about this place is that all kinds of people come in. The thing we have in common is we're all poor. But I don't really want that in common with them, so that's a bad thing.

A couple of five-year-old kids sat in the middle of the floor. "Let's see how long we can hold our breaths," the chubby, pale-faced kid said.

"Okay," said the other kid, jaundiced and thin-looking. Their cheeks puffed out, and both faces began to turn red. The faces looked better than they did with their original colors.

Once in a while, a bleach-blond head poked its way out the hollow wooden door at the side and called the next number. They were on 35. I looked at my ticket. 49. And I'd already been there three hours. I think they try to get you to leave by making you wait so long.

I'd started that annoying habit I have of picking at my fake nails, when the front door opened, and a man in a sleek, tan suit walked in. I guess he was about forty. He was tall and thin and looked like he'd spent a lot of time dressing. He had blond hair, probably the same color the guy next to me would have if he ever washed his. The tall man carried a black leather bag bigger than a briefcase but smaller than a suitcase. He went to the center of the room and just stood there for a minute. He cleared his throat.

"Good afternoon, ladies and gentlemen," he said. His voice was more than simply loud because the room hushed like he had started to strip.

"I'm here to offer you some exceptional values today," he announced. "And I think you should take advantage of them because these are limited items at wholesale prices. What I have here," and he dug into his bag, "is a hi-fi portable music system that will make you feel like you are in the theater."

Everyone just stared at him silently like zombie high school students. He didn't seem to notice, or if he did, he didn't care because he just went on, opening a box.

"This model," he said, carefully pulling out a plain black, plastic, square-looking thing, "is good for traveling and walking. It can be plugged into any stereo system, earphones, or speakers, and has phenomenal sound no matter where you use it. Allow me to demonstrate."

He walked toward a wall with a painted-over outlet. He leaned down and plugged the thing in. Because everyone was now looking at this guy, I could afford to look at him too. For a second, I wondered where he got the equipment anyway.

Gloria finally noticed, but by that time, sounds of ocean waves struck the room. The sounds were kind of nice. He held the stereo thing in his open palm, raising his hand above his head so we could all see where this amazing sound was coming from. A group of people actually got up for a closer look. They were in awe like he was holding up a statue of a god or something.

"Sir!" Gloria bellowed, practically sticking her head under the glass slot that kept the workers separated from people like us. "What are you doing?"

Now people didn't know if they should stare at Gloria or the salesman. I stared at the clock again so I could disappear into my aura of self-importance. I watched from the corner of my eye and listened.

The man ignored her, lowering his hand, messing with the knobs and dials on the sound system. He hummed the classical tune that played behind the ocean waves. The group grew, and some leaned in for a closer look. Gloria leaped from her chair and rounded a corner behind her glass. When she reappeared, it was with a security guard.

The guard was old and had completely white hair, droopy eyes, and nose hairs. He hurried as quickly as he could to the side office door that led to the waiting room. "Excuse me, sir," he called in a shaky voice, much quieter than Gloria's.

"Sir." He made his way through the spectators and closer to the huckster. "Sir!" he said louder this time.

The huckster finally turned. "Hello," he said. "Can I interest you in this sound system? I sell at wholesale prices and even offer a guarantee."

"This is a state agency, sir," the guard said rather firmly. "There's no soliciting here."

The ocean waves crashed. The violins sang. The security guard reached over to the salesman's hand and turned off the mini stereo.

"Oh," said the salesman. It was quiet in there now. He honestly looked sad. I kind of felt bad for him. "Well, I'm sorry then. I don't suppose you know anyone else who might be interested?"

"No, sir, I do not," said the guard. "Now, please leave."

I wondered if the guy was going to give the guard any trouble, but he didn't.

The group of spectators returned to their seats and wall space and floor. The huckster smiled bravely at the crowd, making eye contact with anyone he could. He waved. "Thank you, everyone!" he said. "Have a nice day!"

The glass front door shut.

"Dumb ass," the greasy-haired man next to me murmured. "Goddamn stupid prick."

I didn't say anything, just stared at the clock.

Finally, they called my number.

Drawing by Ron Kendrick

SLEEPING IN ON SATURDAY MORNING

Ron Kendrick

I *brace my body for another wave of pain. It is dark, and I am motionless. I don't remember if I have decided to remain still or if I am unable to move. The pain finally retreats and does not immediately return. I am confused and afraid.*

Swerving abruptly, Sheriff Wilson barely avoids colliding with the wreckage at the bridge. He instinctively turns on his flashing lights and parks his squad car on the edge of the road. He runs back to the bridge to inspect the wreckage. Squinting through the side glass of the mangled, silver sports coupe, he can see dark smears around the nose and mouth of the driver. Both car doors are crumpled. He tries to open the door on the passenger side, but it's jammed into the front fender.

I am running through a rain forest along the banks of a river. A storm rages all around me. I stop running and search the skies. Why am I running? What am I running from? Lightning flashes, again and again. I raise my hand

above my head for protection as I struggle to understand.
Fragments slowly creep into my consciousness. I remember
talking with my father.

After setting flares, the sheriff calls for a rescue squad
and turns his attention back to the crash victim. Flickering
yellows and oranges from the burning flares have turned
the August night into a strange fantasy world.

Suddenly overwhelmed by smells of Kentucky bourbon,
spicy tapas, and floral perfumes, I find myself in a large
noisy room. Floor-to-ceiling glass windows are spaced be-
tween heavy stonework. I know this place. Fear has trans-
formed into a Friday night at Greystone Resort. I allow my-
self to relax a little, thinking that perhaps I can handle this.

Vance Wilson has been the county sheriff for over
twenty years. He has responded to many accidents in this
quiet, rural county of clean air, white caps on rushing rivers,
and thick green forests. The front of the victim's car is
wrapped around one end of the concrete bridge abutment
over Low Dutch Creek. Knowing the nearest ambulance will
take at least thirty minutes to arrive, Vance's immediate
concern is for the victim's survival. He carefully begins
working to open the passenger door with a crowbar. The
driver is not moving and appears to be firmly pinned behind
the steering wheel.

I am exhausted. In my gut I know that we are behind
schedule on my latest project. I need some magic. I have not

slept since last Saturday night. By the third night without sleep, I felt my productivity failing, but I kept pushing. I caught myself fantasizing about reading a good novel on the soft sand of Orient Beach. Distractions are not acceptable during this stage of the project.

Prying open the passenger door, Vance discovers the driver trapped behind the dashboard and the busted steering column. Below the knee, his leg is pinned under the buckled transmission housing. He appears to have lost a lot of blood. Wiping sweat from his own forehead, Vance stretches across the passenger seat and leans closer to the driver.

I know I should not be at this reception, too much work to do. However, after five days without sleep I am feeling invincible. I figure I could make a showing at the party and slip away early. I feel clammy. This is bad because I perspire very easily. Now I am afraid I may start sweating. I can't stop thinking about the work I have to finish after the party.

The victim's eyes are open, and he stares back at Vance. His stare is intense and frightened. Vance sees the eyes of a fighter, aware that the odds are against him. Vance's stomach tightens as he struggles to maintain his focus. The victim's skin feels cold and clammy. The damage inside the car is much worse than he expected. Gently touching the victim's shoulder, Vance attempts to communicate some reassurance.

Is that Dad's hand resting on my shoulder? I can't re-member Dad ever touching my shoulder like that. He shouldn't even be here. This is a geek party. I don't think Dad has been to a party since I was a child and my folks hosted a New Year's Eve celebration. Why is he touching my arm? Displays of physical affection were very rare in my family. I must be hallucinating. I'm not used to drinking bourbon.

"Hey, can you hear me?" It appears the driver either fell asleep or was distracted just as he entered the bridge at the curve in the road. This section of the road does not have a shoulder. His vehicle smashed into the bridge abutment on dead center. Vance pleads, "Can you hear me? Help will be here soon." Slowly backing away, Vance begins to feel a growing attachment to this stranger.

I realize my dad is talking to me. But I can't understand what he is saying. I'm enjoying Dad's company. Is this the same father I knew when I was a kid?

In an attempt to learn more about the victim, Vance moves to the rear of the car and opens the hatch.

While Dad is talking, I have a sudden flash of inspira-tion. Perhaps something he said triggered the idea. I am sud-denly feeling a sense of heady euphoria. If I leave the party now, I can be back at my office by 5 a.m. I briefly wonder if the bourbon has anything to do with my optimism. I decide it is time to abandon this party and return to my lab.

Inside the hatch, Vance discovers a backpack containing an assortment of electronic gadgets. There are also a few business cards that identify Max Davis as a technical director for an engineering company. While looking for emergency-contact information, he is able to determine that Max is twenty-eight years old. It occurs to Vance that if he had a son, he would be about the same age.

It usually takes about two hours to drive to my office from Greystone Resort, but I should make good time, as there is no traffic on the roads at this late hour. As I settle into the cold driver's seat, the sudden chill reminds me of the fall season in Virginia when I was growing up. Dad never turned the heat on until absolutely necessary. Cold would penetrate the old frame structure of the house and chill my body to the backside of my skin. Anticipating warmth from the car heater, I start the engine.

Vance is interrupted by the wailing sound of sirens. An ambulance closely followed by the flashing lights of a tow truck pull in behind the wreckage. Vance quickly updates the rescue squad. He watches closely as they carefully extract Max from his wreckage and carry him to the ambulance. In the back of the ambulance, Vance lightly touches Max on his left wrist. As he does so, a chill passes from Max directly into Vance, causing him to shiver. Vance grabs another blanket and gently places it over Max. He irrationally feels compelled to ride along with Max in the ambulance, as though this would help keep him alive.

I am seventeen years old and waking up on a cold morning in November. It is pre-dawn, and yet I intuitively sense that dawn is getting close. I don't want to get out of bed. I never want to get up that early. It seems as though I have just gone to bed. I usually study well past midnight. No matter, my father always makes sure I get up on time.

I don't want to step onto the cold, wooden floors of my bedroom. I roll onto my side and pull the covers tight around my neck. I am still cold. I have a collection of fantasies that I use to help me sleep. I choose one and let my imagination take over. In my mind I fully embrace the illusion. A wave of warmth surges through my body. Wrapped in this imaginary warmth, I await the sound of my father's voice.

A loud crackling sound from inside the squad car startles Vance. It is Sharon, his dispatcher calling for assistance. Vance is needed to respond to a disturbance at a local roadhouse. He hesitates briefly. He still feels compelled to follow the ambulance to the emergency room and not abandon Max Davis. Nevertheless, remembering his duty, Vance acknowledges Sharon's call.

Something is different this morning. I haven't heard Dad's footsteps on the stairway. He always goes downstairs and starts his morning coffee before he calls. There is no aroma of coffee in the air. Maybe it's much earlier than I think. Perhaps Dad has overslept. That would be a first. I allow myself to drift deeper into the warmth of my fantasy. It feels so good with the covers pulled tight around my neck, safe from the cold air.

Vance watches the ambulance as it disappears down the road into the night mist. He silently wishes the best for Max Davis as he drives off in the opposite direction.

Every touch of morning chill compels me to tightly embrace the softness and warmth under my covers. Perhaps Dad won't call for a while. Just once, maybe I'll sleep as long as I want. I feel warm, secure, and completely relaxed for the first time in my life. Exhaling with a sigh of relief, I surrender.

Dad never calls.

Max Davis sleeps in on Saturday morning.

*   *   *   *   *   *   *

A week later Vance is back at the hospital for the seventh time. He has visited daily since that Friday night at the bridge over Low Dutch Creek.

I am running through a thick rain forest. Bolts of lightning provide the only illumination against the dark sky. I have a sword in my hand. Somehow I know I am running for my life. Racing along the shore of a wide turbulent river, my direction is determined by the lightning bolts. Once again the Goddess is meddling in my life. The lightning strikes so close that I am forced to shield myself with my sword. I know that I am being forced to run out of the rain forest.

I must keep running.

Vance has just stepped into the lounge to take a break when suddenly an alarm sounds throughout the intensive-care ward. A nurse runs to check the patient monitors. Nurse Webb's voice is loud, firm, and clear. "I need help on number seven."

The patient has been comatose for several days. The doctors would not offer a prognosis. When nurse Webb arrives, the formerly comatose patient in room number seven has already removed his IVs and the tube from his throat. She arrives just in time to stop him from removing the plastic catheter from his stomach.

In the morning, she will have to inform Doctor York that one of his patients nearly escaped from intensive care.

Drawing by Ron Kendrick

THE BLUEBERRY FARM

Bette Hileman

It was July 1954. Carol was eighteen. It seemed like an idyllic Monday morning at the Dorset blueberry farm in western Massachusetts. She had arrived at eight. She would start gathering berries as soon as sun dried the dew on the bushes.

Nearly all the local teenage girls who lived year round in Dorset were already at the farm. And two boys whose families had summer homes there had arrived to work in the barn, packing berries. Summer kids from Hartford and New York whose families owned two or three houses were so wealthy they didn't need to work. But maybe, Carol thought, they liked the companionship and independence they gained earning extra money.

Her good friend Karen, who was also eighteen and lived in Dorset, wasn't picking berries this season, though she had every other year since she turned twelve. She was working as a counselor at a Girl Scout camp ten miles away where she was paid more than she could earn on the farm. She needed the money for college.

The views from the farm were beautiful. It was located on the crest of North Street. An old stone wall marked the front boundary of the property. Beyond it stood a row of mature, stout maple trees. Between them, Carol could see fields and distant mountains, a pale misty blue in early morning light.

As always, Carol was wearing a one-piece bathing suit and shorts, just like other young female pickers from Dorset and the neighboring town of Bath. They sat on the lawn in front of the farm owner's house and barn as they waited for dew to evaporate. About fifteen Polish women in their mid-forties were gathered on the lawn as well. Unlike the girls, they wore long-sleeved shirts, ankle-length trousers, and babushkas to protect their heads and necks from sun.

The teenagers considered the older women elderly and quaint, a throwback to the peasant lives their parents had led in Poland. Beginning in early June when so few berries were ripe that picking lasted only two to three hours a day, the women arrived at the farm every morning. And they kept coming to work after school started, gathering berries that ripened until the first frost. The money they earned from berries provided much of their families' incomes. They knew little or no English. They spoke their native language to each other and never uttered a word to anyone else.

At nine, the farm owner, George, called the teenagers from the front door of his 200-year-old, rundown house, telling them in Polish-accented English it was time to start. He also said something in Polish to the older women. The workers quickly ran uphill to the fields behind the house, grabbed flat wooden carriers that each held twelve empty pint boxes, and began picking. Their supervisor, a high school teacher from Bath, told them exactly which bushes to tackle first.

They were paid one dollar for a carrier. After each was filled, they took it to the supervisor, who checked it for leaves and unripe berries and set it in the pickup truck beside the field. If a worker turned in baskets with more than a few leaves or white berries, she would likely lose her job.

Carol considered the job a good one because the money she earned equaled the starting wages of unskilled factory laborers and would provide enough for books and travel expenses at college. Each Friday, she and the other workers queued up and received their pay in cash in small envelopes.

Harvesting blueberries was pleasant. The pickers sat on a deep layer of sawdust that covered the ground around the bushes. The air was warm, but not too hot. The five-foot tall plants provided shade.

Carol loved being at the farm. It gave her a chance to visit with her friends at leisure and hear about experiences very different from her own. She especially enjoyed visiting with Margaret and Tom, whose father owned the farm. Frequently, after work ended at five, she ate supper with them and their mother.

That afternoon, teenage girls from Bath, also dressed in bathing suits and shorts, were gathering berries on bushes near Carol, and she listened to their conversation.

Young men from Dorset often bragged that if they wanted sex, all they had to do was drive ten miles to Bath in the evening and pick up one of several girls who were ambling on the sidewalks. Carol doubted those stories, thinking the boys were trying to appear desirable by inventing escapades with Bath girls. She also felt they were subtly telling the Dorset females they were too uptight because none even considered wandering the streets and making herself available to a stranger. How could a girl just get in a car with someone she didn't know who stopped near the sidewalk and have sex with him a few hours later? Carol wondered.

But that afternoon, she learned some of the stories were true. Marcy who was working on a bush near Carol was bragging about her experiences with an exciting young man from Dorset.

"I was walking to the grocery store," Marcy said, "and he pulled up in a nice pickup."

"What did he say?" asked Jane, one of Marcy's companions.

"He said, 'Do you want a ride home?' I replied, 'Sure.' My house was just half a mile away. But I thought, 'Why not?'"

"Then what happened?"

"We went for a long ride and ended up at the lake. You know the one in the quarry. His kisses and fucking were so nice," Marcy said loud enough so everyone on neighboring bushes could hear. All the girls, including those from Dorset, were quiet as they waited to learn more.

"Will you see him again?" Jane said.

"Don't know. Maybe when he gets lonely. I don't care. There are other boys. Hardly a day goes by when someone doesn't try to give me a ride."

"I know what you mean."

"The ones from Dorset. They're the best."

The older women working a few feet away continued their banter in Polish, seemingly unaware of Marcy's revelation. Carol wished Karen were there so she could discuss the story with her. She hadn't talked with her all summer because the camp had only one phone, which was used by the director. The Bath girls, who were listening to Marcy's tale as they worked nearby, were giggling. They didn't appear shocked, or even surprised, by it. Most were good looking—very tan, many with blond hair bleached even blonder by the sun. They had thin waists and ample breasts and had removed their bathing suit straps so their backs would tan evenly.

Carol wanted to feel as carefree, at least for a day or two, as the Bath girls appeared. She wished she could lose her fears of pregnancy or rape or loss of reputation. None of the Bath girls seemed to worry about the future. They weren't aiming to prepare themselves for college or any profession.

After Marcy turned to more boring topics, Carol began talking with her friends. This summer they had been reading John Steinbeck's novels at home and discussing them at work. They found *Grapes of Wrath* especially exciting and compared the characters' experiences with their own. Though Carol and her friends didn't live in squalid conditions like those in *Grapes of Wrath*, they often found joy in farm work and natural surroundings, as did Steinbeck's characters.

In mid-afternoon, Carol started walking toward the barn to take a break. When she reached the edge of the field, the farm owner's daughter Margaret, who was two years older, approached her and whispered, "Did you hear what happened to Karen?"

"No," Carol said with a sense of dread. No one could hear their conversation because she and Margaret were standing far from the other workers.

"She was gang-raped on Saturday night."

"What?" Carol said, suddenly afraid. "How could it happen?"

"At a party the teenage Girl Scout counselors organized for themselves. They invited about a dozen college boys who summer nearby on Echo Lake and some other young people from Dorset. They held the party in an abandoned cabin on the lake."

"How did you find out about it?"

"My brother Tom and I were there. No parents or older adults attended."

"Wasn't there anything you could do to stop it?" Carol said quietly, trying not to sound accusatory. She didn't want to alienate Margaret.

"No, some of the boys went crazy. There was no way to interfere."

"How many?" Carol asked, fearing an answer.

"Five. You know them. Guys whose parents have summer places at the lake. Smith and Arms boys."

Carol had met them at parties their families held but didn't know them well. Their parents were rumored to be alcoholics, and she assumed the boys drank a lot too.

"Why? What brought it on?"

"Karen was drunk. She passed out."

Carol was devastated. One impulse was to remain silent so she wouldn't have to learn more. She couldn't understand why Margaret—an intelligent, beautiful woman—didn't seem upset by what she'd revealed. But then, Margaret always viewed disturbing situations calmly.

"What happened afterward?" Carol said.

"Tom and I took her home. Even in the car, she remained almost unconscious. We carried her into the house."

"Do her parents know about it?"

"I don't think so. Karen wouldn't have told them. It would have upset them too much. All they likely know is she got drunk at the party."

"This is *awful*. What's going to happen to Karen?"

"Probably nothing," Margaret said soothingly, trying to reassure Carol.

"Can't she go to the police?"

"It would accomplish nothing, except make her reputation even worse. They would consider her at fault because she was drunk."

"No girl is really responsible for rape."

"That's not how the police and courts think. Besides Karen's parents are too poor to hire a lawyer. The boys are wealthy, so they would fight charges tooth and nail."

"Do you think she could be pregnant?"

"Probably not. Rape doesn't usually cause pregnancy."

"Maybe not. But it does happen."

Margaret turned and ambled toward the barn.

Carol walked slowly back to work. For the next two hours, as she continued gathering berries, she was pensive, thinking about what Margaret had told her, but trying to behave as if nothing unusual had happened. Two girls from Dorset were sitting near her, picking on the same bush. Carol didn't say anything about the rape. She didn't want to damage Karen's reputation more by telling her friends about it.

After five, when the workers had gone home, Carol went into the barn where the pints of blueberries were inspected for leaves and unripe berries, covered with cellophane, and packed in wooden crates for shipment to New York City. Tall stacks of crates filled with berries stood near the huge barn door and in a long row beside the processing table. No one was there except Margaret's brother Tom, who was Carol's age. Tall and muscular with light brown hair, he had penetrating, deep-set, blue eyes. She had known him since first grade and had always been attracted to him.

"Did you hear what happened to Karen?" Tom said cheerfully. His tone was the same as it might have been if he were asking about the latest Red Sox scores or whether she'd seen a new movie at the drive-in in Eastfield. But his face looked tense and drawn as if he were trying to conceal emotion.

"I heard. Your sister told me," Carol said, wanting to scream. She wondered how Tom could speak with nonchalance about the incident when he, too, was one of Karen's close friends.

"Why didn't you call the police?" Carol asked. "Was there no phone in the cabin? Couldn't you have interfered?"

"There was no phone. We couldn't stop it. The boys went wild. Besides, calling the police would have made things worse for Karen. There would have been a scandal, and everyone for miles around would have heard about it."

Carol tried to imagine what he meant by "boys going wild." Did that imply crazy, unstoppable? She was too upset to say anything more. Tears streamed down her cheeks. She quickly crawled behind the crates along the processing table and crouched down behind the tall stack near the large open door, trying to hide her face. She was afraid Tom would consider her weak or childish if he saw her tears. In the twelve years he'd known her, he'd never seen her cry. She didn't want to lose his friendship or respect now.

Tom walked slowly around the barn interior, searching for her. Finally, he saw her. He bent down and looked directly at her face. His expression changed from blankness to one of sympathy and concern.

"Are you okay?" he said. "I didn't mean to upset you."

"I'm okay. But it's not *me* we need to worry about. I'm trying to figure out if there is anything we can do to help Karen," she said almost in a whisper.

"I don't know. I'll try to think of something."

Tom looked at Carol with tenderness. She felt he realized how devastating the rape was for her and perhaps how awful it must have been for Karen. He didn't know that on a first date three summers ago, a boy from Dorset tried to attack Carol in the woods. Even though she didn't plan to reveal that to Tom, she believed he was aware of her feelings. She was deeply grateful, but still didn't know what, if anything, she could do to help Karen.

Drawing by Ron Kendrick

NOWHERE UNLIMITED

Katherine Mercurio Gotthardt

If she was going to be bed-bound, she might at least like her characters.

It was one thing to run out of plot, but it was another to loathe her protagonists by the second page and grudgingly drag her writing behind their limping lead.

Stunted writer Serendipity thought her newest character, Claire, particularly annoying. She did things that made Serendipity want to scratch out her own eyeballs with a steel brush. For example, Claire smoked Marlboros, unfiltered, and tapped her feet to the drumbeat of classic rock.

When her legs felt cramped from driving, Claire, bent-kneed, crammed her left one over the speaker, muddying the heat vent as her work boots pressed against the grid—all while still driving.

Claire caterwauled with the radio. She bleached her hair and wore blue eye shadow. How could anyone tolerate this woman?

If it weren't for dialysis slam-dunking Serendipity into a treatment funk, she thought she could at least exercise away her angst and her grudge against Claire.

Maybe fifteen minutes of running in place would cure her of asking, "What should this bitch do next?"

But Serendipity knew right down to her rotting liver that working up a good sweat, even one not illness-induced, would not make her a better writer.

She tried reading contemporary novels, tried copying the styles of best-selling authors. She tried to let her characters do what they wanted, as wise and popular fiction authors recommended. She read the market and writing self-help books. She registered and completed an online writing course. She hired a professional editor whose feedback diluted her ego even more: "Your characters are too generic. Give them some more quirks."

Hence, Claire smoked Marlboros, unfiltered, and tapped her feet to the drumbeat of classic rock.

Wasn't that quirky enough?

But where was Claire driving, and why?

Presumably, she was trying to escape the vampire that had followed her through three faceless cities. Claire was on the run, but Serendipity couldn't tell if Claire's driving habits were brought on by a lackadaisical nature or nervousness. And if she, the author, couldn't tell, how could the reader?

Serendipity rested her head back on the damp pillow. She closed her eyes. Her fingers napped on the keys of the laptop. Maybe a dream would set her imagination free and the vampire would make Claire more interesting. Vampires could do that, right? At least being undead was somewhat unique. Or was it?

It seemed Claire could do only two things: flee from city to city and drive. Yes, Claire was stuck in an endless, blood-sucking cycle that put rubber to the road with an occasional screech of tires erupting from the 1978 Ford pickup.

The pickup lacked power brakes and power steering. Claire had the strength to turn the wheel when absolutely necessary, which was possibly one redeeming quality. But sometimes, in the fugue and fatigue of driving, she just couldn't get herself to press that brake pedal.

Without opening her eyes, Serendipity clicked the keys.

Claire slammed into a vein-clad oak.

Beside the bed, a dialysis machine churned.

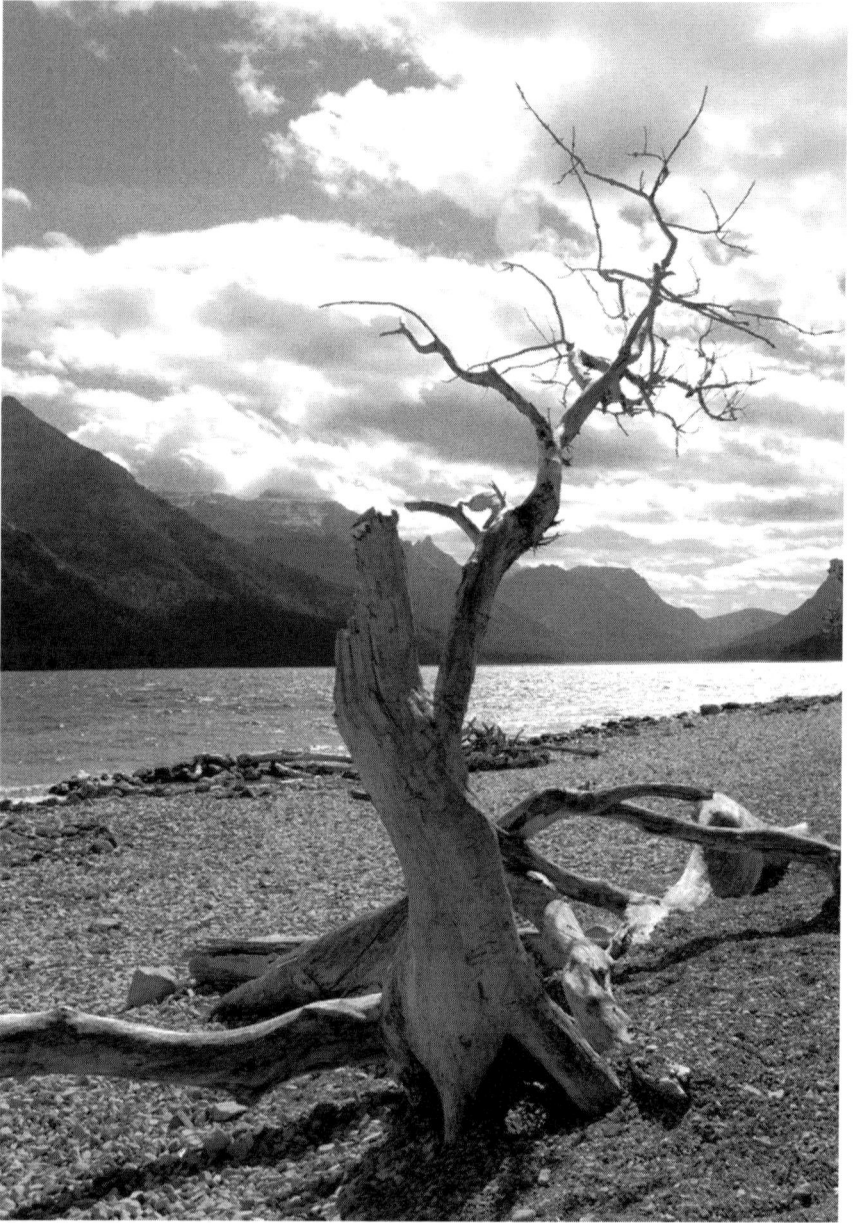

Photo by Bette Hileman

THE LAST TREE

Larry S. Underwood

Once upon a time . . . Many stories start "once upon a time." And usually when they do, they take us back.

Back to a time when something happened. Something the story wants us to remember.

This story starts "once upon a time," but it takes us forward in time. Forward, to an event that has not happened yet. To an event that may happen, though, in the days of our great-grandchildren's great-grandchildren.

Once upon a time, in that time, there was a great city. For as far as the eye could see the city stretched. Nothing but buildings and glass and concrete for as far as the eye could see. And roadways and walkways and subways—the roar of engines and the hum of motors, and the bleat of horns and the incessant babble of people. For as far as the mind could stretch, the city stretched. It was a great city. Everyone said so.

There were no green plants in this city. Except for one. In the very center of the city, completely surrounded by buildings, roadways, and people, there was one last tree. It was a huge old tree—twisted, gnarled, and nearly as tall as the buildings. I don't know what miracle had occurred to allow this tree to be spared when all the others were cut down, but that miracle had occurred. And there it was. In the middle of the city. One last tree.

There were no animals in this city. Except, of course, for the people. There were millions and millions of people. But they, it seemed, were all sick. They went to their doctors and complained of a variety of ills. And the doctors prescribed a variety of pills, salves, and ointments that the people took as scheduled. But the medicines did no good. So the doctors prescribed special diets that the people ate faithfully. But the diets did no good. So the doctors designed special exercise plans that the people followed religiously. But the exercise did no good. The people were still sick. And the doctors could not make them well.

Except for one doctor. He told all his patients:

"Go to the tree in the center of the city. Go and simply spend time with the tree. Breathe in its presence. Smell the fragrance of its leaves and blossoms. Put your arms 'round the tree. Press your cheek against its bark. Feel its roughness. Squeeze the tree tightly. Feel its great strength. Do it and it will make you well."

"Well," the people thought, "this seems a little weird. But nothing else has worked. Why not?"

And so they tried it.

They went to the tree, as directed. They spent time with the tree. They breathed in its presence. They put their arms 'round the tree, pressed their cheeks against its bark, and felt its roughness. They squeezed the tree tightly and felt its great strength.

And, lo, it worked! The people instantly felt better. Why, they actually felt well! The people who had hugged the tree felt well!

It didn't last, of course. The people still lived in the city. And soon they felt as sick as they ever had. So, back they went to their doctor.

"It was wonderful for a while. But it didn't last. What do we do now?"

"Go back to the tree," the doctor told them. "You can go to the tree as often as you need to. And it will make you well."

And so they did. Whenever they felt a little bad, they went to the tree. Some went once a month. Some went once a week. Some even went every day. And it never failed to make them feel better.

Now, the doctor had quite a few patients. And he sent them all to the tree. Soon there were lots of people gathered 'round the tree. And other doctors, seeing how successful the first doctor was, started sending their patients to the tree as well. Soon there were lots more people 'round the tree. Soon there were so many people 'round the tree that lines had to form. And sometimes people had to wait, sometimes for quite a while.

And still more people came. Soon there were so many people that the lines were always there. And the delays got longer and longer. Soon they were bringing people to the tree in busloads. Soon there were so many people trying to spend time with the tree that a law had to be passed. And the law said that no one could spend more than fifteen minutes at a time with the tree. And still the people came. More and more people. Soon they had to pass another law. And this law said that no one could spend more than one minute at a time with the tree. And still more and more people came. From all over the city, they came. Soon there were so many people crowding 'round the tree that no one could get next to the tree.

And no one could get well.

And that is the end of the story.

It is a story that has not happened yet. But it may happen in the days of our great-grandchildren's great-grandchildren. And as they stand in those long, long lines, I imagine they will think back to this time and they will say:

"How wonderful it would have been to live in those days when there were so many trees. Do you realize that in those days there were more trees than people? Why, in those days everyone could have had their own tree to hug."

Listen to the words of our great-grand children's great-grandchildren:

"Ancient ones, know how lucky you were to have lived in a time when there were so many trees. Honor your trees. Cherish your trees. And every chance you get, spend time with a tree. Breathe in its presence. Smell the fragrance of its leaves and blossoms. Put your arms around the tree.

Press your cheek against its bark and feel its roughness. Hug your tree tightly and feel its great strength."

Those are the words of our great-grandchildren's great-grandchildren.

Inspired by an essay by Thich Nhat Nanh

Drawing by Ron Kendrick

THE RIGHT TO LAUGH

Katherine Mercurio Gotthardt

December D.C. air does not welcome the stranger unaccustomed to cold.

Estefan drew the baggy Berber jacket closer to his ribs, merging neck and head with collar, like a turtle hoping a thin shell would serve as environmental protection.

But he did manage a laugh.

Laughing was a commodity, no matter how rusty. But having made it to Washington, Estefan had earned the right to laugh in partial victory and partial irony, no matter how quickly that laugh was doused in the clamor of icy wind.

The laugh surprised him. He supposed it must be as the Americans said: "Just like riding a bike." You don't forget how to do it.

The bikes Estefan had ridden in his lifetime outnumbered the times he had laughed.

A bicycle may or may not help now, Estefan thought, surveying the once-muddy walkway alongside the National Mall. The frozen footprints of politicos and fossilized horseprints of mounted police could prove hazardous even for a mountain bike. While he had ridden over Texas-bound rough terrain and through Houston streets rigged with pot-holes, winter pitfalls like those at the mall should be avoided. Better to trudge in his new hiking boots. Get his money's worth, since that footwear had nearly emptied his pockets.

The Washington Monument might have impressed him more had the water stretching toward it not been petrified by the elements, had the day offered at least thirty more degrees—though forty or fifty or sixty would be ideal—and had he more than three dollars in his jeans pocket.

While arriving penniless in the country's capital might allow him to fit in with the pressing numbers of street peo-ple, it would not keep him from starving or freezing to death. At least in Texas, spreading gravel and slopping ce-ment in warmer weather had earned him enough to buy beef, peppers, and tomatoes. It was more than he would have here, he suspected.

Canvases, paintbrushes, charcoal, soft erasers, pig-ment—out of the question. His last portrait had sold for what equaled fifteen dollars to a proud new father of a girl with a head full of black hair.

Estefan had been pleased. In the backcountry of Guate-mala, that money would feed him for days and buy him art supplies for months. He wondered what he might paint here had he the money. Did street artists earn enough to live?

His feet had been moving automatically, partly as a sur-vival instinct, partly because he knew temporary shelter would not be found near Constitution Avenue unless he were seeking an iced bench. No, four, five, six blocks past classical columns, slick marble, carvings of lions, and the scales of justice, into the real city, and he might find what he needed.

Estefan knew how to move quickly. He also knew that when, more than five miles into his trek he happened across a child's lost scarf, he'd best wear it, even though it barely tied beneath his grizzled chin and even though it sported a grinning, yellow appliqué of Sponge Bob.

He wore the cartoon on the inside.

MEMOIR

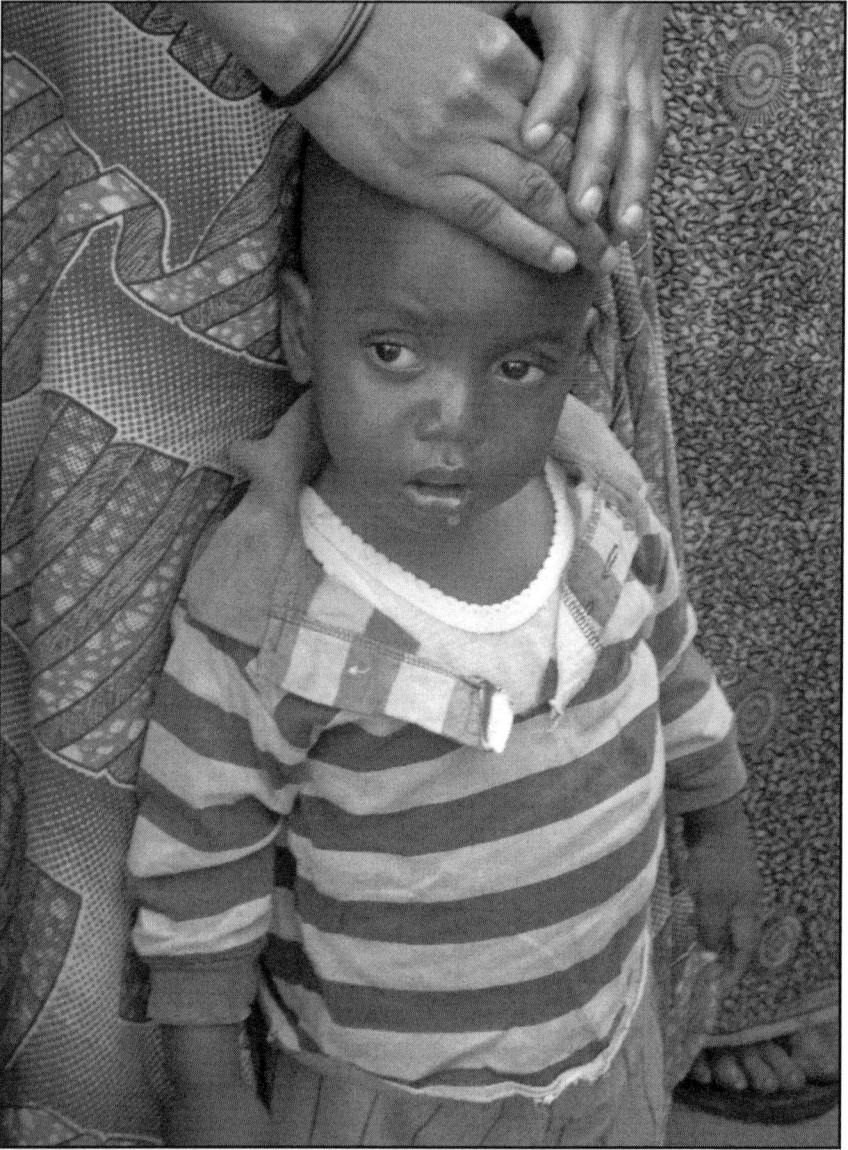

Photo by Coleen Kivlahan

VISITING THE MISSIONARIES

Steve Clapp

When I was a Peace Corps volunteer in Nigeria in 1963, I spent a month helping primary school teachers in Dapchi, a remote village in the far north of the country. The nearest town was forty miles away.

"Why don't you take a trip to Gashua?" my Peace Corps supervisor suggested during his visit to me in Dapchi. "It would be a good break. There are some missionaries there. You could stay with them."

"Shouldn't I let them know beforehand?" I asked.

"Out here? This is bush. You don't need to be formal out here. What are you going to do? Send a calling card by lorry and wait for a reply? Just show up. They'll be happy to see somebody—especially you, since you're a minister's son."

It did seem like a good idea, so on Thursday afternoon I packed some things and walked down to the lorry station. The sky clouded over, rain threatened, and I was about to give up when the man in charge said a lorry would come about five.

It was close to seven when the lorry actually got under way. I was sitting on a wooden seat in the *gabah*, the cab, with the driver and his assistant. My bag was back in the *bodi* with several sacks of groundnuts and about a dozen other passengers.

Photo by Steve Clapp

We slogged over the rain-dampened road, pausing to meet plorries coming in the other direction. Occasionally, a bell would ring in the cab. This was a signal from somebody in the bodi that another lorry wished to pass. We would crawl off the road and allow ourselves to be overtaken.

I was quite sore from sitting on the wooden seat by the time we arrived in Gashua around nine. I asked for the *gidan Bature* (the Europeans' house), and I was directed to the home of a Sudan Interior Missionary (SIM) named Worling.

Worling's affiliation with the SIM, which was prevalent in Nigeria, stirred some misgivings. My Peace Corps housemate, a divinity school dropout, called SIM missionaries "fundies," but my previous experiences with missionaries had been pleasant, so I had no idea what was in store.

Then, too, anyone—fundamentalist or not—might be less than charitable to a stranger who knocked on his door at 9:30 p.m. It was with a mixture of relief and apprehension that I greeted Mr. Worling, who had been reading by kerosene lamp, and introduced myself.

To enter the Worling living room was to enter pre-war America. Little had changed since the couple had come to Gashua in 1938. The woodwork was dark, the furniture plain. A metal sign, "Jesus Never Fails," hung above their bedroom door.

George Worling was a man of medium build—on the smallish side, actually—with graying hair and a face whose aspect was curiously open and cheerful. We spent the next few minutes feeling each other out. I figured that a few key phrases, such as "Peace Corps" and "Congregational minister's son," would soon establish rapport. Instead, I found myself increasingly on the defensive.

"Congregationalist, huh?" said Mr. Worling. "Ever hear of the Park Street Church in Boston? Ever hear Rev. Ockengay preach? He's quite a preacher, you know."

I recognized the Park Street Church as a bastion of conservatism in an otherwise liberal denomination.

About this time Mrs. Worling had finished making up my bed and wanted to share the tea and ice cream George had fixed. "This is Mr. Clapp, Sue," said George. "He's with Kennedy's Peace Corps—teaching down in Dapchi, aren't you? He heard we have good beds and food over here."

"Pleased to meet you," said Sue. "Maybe you can tell me what this Peace Corps is all about. Is it a social scheme or what?"

"Yes, it's a social scheme," George said before I could reply. I discovered that "social," in the Worling vocabulary, was short for "socialist."

I thought I might have some luck charming Sue, George having proven a pretty tough nut to crack. Sue, however, was even tougher. She struck me as a curiously American phenomenon: a woman whom virtue, or something like it, had made hard and cynical. In her vision of the world, the evil prosper and the "saved" are doomed to misfortune.

Her lack of charity extended even to her daughters. "Millie's trying to get another degree at Oklahoma State," she said. "That's what everybody's doing these days. I guess the end of the world is near."

"How's that?" I asked.

"You know what it says in the Bible," she said. "In the last days, there will be a great seeking after knowledge. That's what everybody wants these days—knowledge and more knowledge!"

"Well, that's certainly true," I answered, happy at last to be able to agree with something the others said.

My campaign with Sue was further compromised by co-incidence. I, the pagan vagabond, had arrived on the evening before her birthday and was doomed to share this special day with her.

I didn't want to pick any quarrels over religion. In fact, I bent over backwards to avoid biting the hand that was feeding me. But the further I retreated, the faster George and Sue pursued. What did I think of Jonathan Edwards and his sermon, "Sinners in the hands of an angry God"? Did I like to listen to fiery preaching?

When it wasn't direct questioning, it was a wearying one-way discussion with George in which I found myself nodding at all kinds of preposterous statements in order to avoid a quarrel.

And I didn't want to quarrel, really. Their situation was bitter enough without my adding to the bitterness. For thirty years they had devoted themselves to preaching to Muslims, whom they didn't respect. "It's just another kind of paganism, as far as I'm concerned," said George.

What satisfaction could there be for them? Their converts were but a handful. "I've seen a lot of people die without accepting Christ," said George. If the number of converts had ever threatened to become large, the Worlings would have certainly been asked to leave. Their one concession to the social gospel was a morning dispensary in which Sue handed out pills and injections to about one hundred people, but this was clearly subordinate to the preaching.

So they had turned their energies inward, praying for themselves and other SIM missionaries and converts and uttering prayers that resembled curses for these "bigoted Muslims" and "godless pagans." Like most people who believe the world is soon coming to an end, they did so because they had little to gain by its continuance. They lived for heaven, where they would meet a God who would embrace them while sending the unrepentant to hell.

I escaped the morning prayer meeting by going into town to run some errands. When I returned, however, I found the SIM forces had been strengthened by the addition of a Miss Janet of Iowa, the Worlings' neighbor and partner. Janet was a big-boned woman in her early forties—not unattractive, really, with a soft face, hair pulled back into a bun and a somewhat distracted look that became focused and impassioned only when she began talking about religion. To a greater degree than the others, she discussed salvation with a matter-of-factness that other women use in recounting surgeries.

"The night my brother died in that automobile accident—it was about a year after I had been saved—I remember I had a feeling that something was wrong," she said during lunch. "And do you know, Sue, I prayed for everyone at home. Yes, I prayed to God to help them at home. And suddenly I had this feeling of peace. Yes, I felt peace, and I knew that everything was all right. I just knew that my brother had made his peace with God and was saved."

After lunch everyone had a nap, and after the nap, tea. I was about to put away my teacup and reach for an old magazine when George plumped "The Evangelist's Hymnbook" in my lap. "We usually have a prayer meeting at this time," he explained. I decided I'd better grin and bear it. They let me have my first choice of hymns, and I demurred.

"Do you know 233?" asked George. I said I didn't. I didn't know 235 either, a "good one" proposed by Janet. I did acknowledge acquaintance with 234, "Come Thou Almighty King." Sue said they didn't know that one too well. So we sang 233, one line of which I remember: "Dear Jesus, wilt thou love such a miserable worm as I?"

George read a Bible passage—something about unbelievers and their fate, slyly intended, no doubt, to bring me around. Next was a prep period for the prayers. George handed out assignments: "Let's see, today we're supposed to pray for that little girl down in Mutum Biu. Oh, yes, and those people in the Somali. Can you think of anything else, Sue?"

Sue couldn't, and at a signal that I failed to catch, all three missionaries whirled from their seats, knelt on the floor, and buried their faces in the seat cushions. I was left, somewhat dumbfounded, staring at Sue's ample backside as she knelt. George led off the prayers, Sue followed, and Janet was anchor. There followed an awkward silence, which I filled with a quiet "Amen."

Apart from all this religiosity, the Worlings were very hospitable and kind. George took me around to meet the emir, whom he grudgingly admired, and the school manager and headmaster. The emir was a rotund, affable, well-educated man who spoke excellent English and had recently received money from the United States for leprosy control. George, whose command of Hausa was such that he preached in the language, could talk with the emir in both Hausa and English.

In the Worlings' house I was treated to two nights on a firm mattress and a profusion of food: biscuits and jam, eggs, hot cereal, Kool-Aid, pigeons, duck, chicken, ice cream, potato chips, and popcorn. The latter treats were served up at Sue's birthday picnic in the evening at a spot overlooking a lake just outside of town.

The party included a Cypriot couple, who were store owners, and the bank manager, an Englishman in his twenties. The Englishman and the Cypriot had shotguns, which they used in vain on lines of ducks and geese flying overhead. The rest of us watched the setting sun, the ducks, the geese, and flocks of pelicans, storks and hornbills streaming across the sky.

When the last of the birthday cake had been eaten, everyone, including Sue herself, was ready for a parlor game. Everyone, that is, except George. "Have you forgotten what day it is?" he asked. "This is the fourth Friday of the month—it's SIM prayer night."

Well, that drove the Cypriots and the Englishman away pretty quickly. Even Janet and Sue seemed to have difficulty working up enthusiasm. But soon we were back in the living room with the hymnbooks and another mimeographed schedule of people to pray for. Things went pretty much according to form, except that George, in a burst of charity, included my family in his prayer.

Morning came. I said goodbye to Sue and stepped across the way to bid farewell to Janet. "Well, all the best in your work," I said, turning to go.

"Yes, and all the best to you, Stephen," she said. "And I mean the really best. You know what that is, don't you, Stephen?" Her face was beautified by a look that, on another woman, would have seemed shamelessly flirtatious.

"Well, yes, I think I do."

"I think you do know, Stephen. Yes, it's Jesus, isn't it? He's really the best. He's the only one who satisfies. I mean nothing else really does satisfy, does it?"

"I suppose not."

"Oh, I think you know in your heart that he's the one who satisfies. I mean, do you know that if you died tonight you would meet your Savior?"

I finally tore myself away after she had pressed a handful of tracts on me. It was a relief to drive away with George, who was much easier to take when he wasn't with his women. There was talk of writing a letter to my family in Connecticut. I wonder if it was done and what it said.

This story is adapted from Africa Remembered: Adventures in Post-Colonial Nigeria and Beyond, *a Peace Corps memoir published by Steve Clapp.*

Drawing by Ron Kendrick

PIANOMANIA

Sheila School

I finally got that baby grand piano out of my life. It took more than thirty years, five or six house moves, and the reality of possibly thousands of dollars in charges to make it playable, but it finally went out my door five years ago—never to return again.

My former husband Paul thought like an engineer, financial expert, and part-time furniture refinisher. He followed a *Cleveland Plain Dealer* classified ad for a "baby grand piano-cheap" to the ice-cold garage of a discouraged fellow do-it-yourselfer. This fellow had removed part of the finish, but had given up on the mammoth job of refinishing the whole large piano. Paul bought the piano for about twenty-five dollars and joyously trailered it home behind his green 1963 Volkswagen bug.

"Look what I found, Honey," he said, smiling.

I looked at the piano with covetous eyes. I really missed having a piano in the house, and scenes of relaxing hours spent at the piano ran through my head.

"That's wonderful, dear. How is the inside of it—does it play?"

"Sure—it has keys and strings and everything. I am going to refinish it. It will be absolutely gorgeous!" he replied.

Right there the ying and yang of marital miscommunication should have hit me over the head. I trusted him that eventually I would have a piano to play. He focused on having a beautiful piano to look at. That these two different goals might be incompatible did not occur to me.

In the first warm days of spring that year, I came home from my job as a music teacher to an unwelcome surprise. To my dismay, the dismembered parts of the piano were now scattered on newspapers all over the back yard.

"What in the devil are you doing to that piano?"

"I told you—I am going to refinish it."

"Paul, I would like to be able to play this piano some day, and it upsets me to see it spread out like that, open to rain, sun, and who knows what else. Are you sure you know what you are doing?"

"Don't worry about it, Hon. The inside of the piano is protected inside the garage and the side surrounding the strings is already stripped. These are just the parts I have to strip and refinish. I can't very well use that finish stripper inside the house, can I? It smells to high heaven and is very toxic. I have a tarp and newspapers to protect the parts. It will be fine."

By then, I was used to Paul when he was on a project. He had lists and lists of lists entered in priority order. He was like a programmed missile, relentless and methodical. Nothing and no one, including me, could stop him once he was launched on something he wanted to do. Meals, conversations, daily hellos and goodbyes were ignored, as were any objections.

The long process of removing the heavy finish, sanding the massive pieces of piano, and deciding on colors and number of coats went on into July, August, and September. Our mailman, who had never seen anybody take a piano apart before and live to tell the tale, closely monitored its progress.

I continued to worry to myself that by the time Paul, rain, heat, and remover gunk was done with, there would be no piano left to play. Finally in late September, all the finishing was done, and it was time to reassemble the piano in our long narrow living room. There it stood in all its gleaming brown and black glory.

"It's absolutely beautiful, dear," I murmured. "Can I play it now?"

"Well," Paul replied, "it may be a little out of tune."

That turned out to be a gross understatement. What issued from the reassembled piano was nothing remotely resembling music. I shouted with frustration "You have completely ruined it!"

I demanded a piano tuner. Instead, Paul, always intent on cheaper solutions to problems, invested in a tuning fork and dug out his set of wrenches. We started on what turned out to be hours of trying to tune the piano. We relied on my ear as to which tone was right, and Paul plied the tuning fork and his various wrenches.

As the resident musician of the house, I finally had enough. "If you won't let me call an expert, you can work on it yourself. Piano tuning is an art, and neither of us understands the first thing about it," was my final word.

So the beautifully restored but unplayable piano sat in that living room, was moved by Paul through two houses in Lexington, three houses in the Washington, D.C., area, and finally to our first purchased house in the Mt. Vernon area of Fairfax County. When Paul moved it into our new house, using the usual rented piano dolly, he broke one of its legs when pushing it up the front staircase. There, the lovely objet d'art rested on its side, threatening the curious amblings of our then one-year-old baby Rowland. Paul refused to do anything about fixing the leg or setting the piano upright. He was now into different lists and lists of lists.

With the support of my mother-in-law, who was visiting, I surreptitiously contacted a piano expert who fixed the leg and hauled the piano to a safer and upright position. Paul was furious, as he did not believe in hiring anyone to do anything in our house. Mom School and I were victorious— for once—and Baby Rowland was safe from being crushed by the now-permanent but useless piano.

From then on, the piano stood and stood and stood, unused, for another twenty-five or so years through a divorce and my move to my present house in Lake Ridge, Virginia. Paul died in 2002, and Rowland, now grown up, moved into our old house and wanted more room in the living room still dominated by the large baby-grand piano. Did I want the piano?

I had the piano moved into my new home and hired an expert to explore the idea of making the piano playable. He advised against it, citing thousands of dollars in restringing and rekeying just to fix the piano. He said it probably wasn't worth doing.

I thought about the thirty-plus years when I'd had no piano to play, weighed the expense of fixing the baby grand, and decided to buy a used, spinet Yamaha piano that would fit easily in my family room. Rowland and I persuaded the piano dealer to take the baby grand off my hands with the possibility of using it in a house-decorating display because it was so beautifully refinished. So my long-time wish for a playable piano was finally fulfilled, and to this day I still enjoy it.

DOODLES

Davis Chung

Our main computer instructor Myron was absent. He was not having problems with motivation or illegal substances. The problem was his son: The fifteen-year-old never showed up at school the previous Friday. It was 1999, and I was working in a small training institute where I helped people who had struggled with life. My function was to help them prepare for passing the general educational development (GED) test. The other section of our school provided basic to intermediate computer skills.

The day before, Myron had asked for help in locating the missing-child website that had the photo of his son. We had silently watched as the image of his boy slowly filled the screen. Being single and childless, I had no frame of reference for the pain and anxiety Myron now endured. Seeing the feelings manifested on his face helped me overlook the incongruity of a computer instructor asking for assistance searching on a computer. Emotions of sadness and longing overflowed from his powerful frame, a physique the ancient Athenian sculptor of the same name would have gladly carved. Behind tinted glasses, Myron's eyes twitched.

"Cheese Doodles?" I offered. They were on sale, and in

my weakness, I had bought two bags. He thanked me and took a handful, while the remaining information downloaded. We made small talk, ate, and printed copies of the photo that he could post around town. I mentally said some prayers for his son's safe return.

The next day, Myron called and asked to speak with me. He thanked me for the help I rendered, the kind words, and the Cheese Doodles. The Cheese Doodles? I thought he misspoke or was joking, but he was serious. As Myron battled his emotions, it seems that, in addition to orange fingertips, he'd also received some minor comfort from the snack. The sharing of food between friends, even something as mundane as an unhealthy food-like substance, seems to have had an effect that escaped my notice.

This was a good reminder of the power to be found in simplicity. It also reminded me that, as a human, my power is limited. The boy was still missing, and nothing I could do would change that. However, there were some things I could do, and though they might have seemed small to me, for those in need, they could seem far greater. Thankfully, after only one more week of waiting, Myron's son was safely returned home.

Drawing by Erika Mooney

VERY DEEP IN DEEP CREEK LAKE

Sheila School

My former husband Paul wanted a boat. In the Sixties in Cleveland Heights, Ohio, where we lived, boats were popular with the younger crowd. After all, we lived right next to Lake Erie, which was feared for its treacherous shallow water. However, Paul was determined to learn to sail and was supremely confident that he could handle any body of water, even Lake Erie.

He decided what we really needed was a portable boat we could store in the basement. After researching camping magazines and attending the local boat show, Paul announced he had found the perfect boat for us—the German-made Klepper. The boat arrived in giant cardboard boxes with its many component parts packed in long, khaki canvas bags fitted with knapsack-like straps. The Klepper was designed for gung-ho European campers to carry on their backs as they portaged from one roaring river to another.

Unfortunately, the Klepper was a craft only a dedicated river runner or a slightly crazy engineer could love. It had to be rebuilt before each use. Paul loved anything that had to be built, fixed, upgraded, or maintained. I was used to standard rowboats and canoes. I had learned boat safety as a camper during several summers in New Hampshire. I deliberately avoided learning to sail while a camper because skidding along sideways in the water did not appeal to me.

The boat began to take shape in our large living room. First, Paul built the complicated rib structure. Next, he stretched the blue neoprene skin over the ribs, pulled it tight, and pumped air into the tubes along the sides of the kayak. He then slid the jib and mainsail in place. The completed Klepper, which turned out to be a very long kayak with two full-sized sails, took up a good part of the living room.

Paul had no experience with boats, but he was never one to let ignorance stand in the way of something he wanted to do. He took his usual tack and proceeded to teach himself to sail by buying a book on the subject and studying it from cover to cover. The only problem with that approach was that, like flying an airplane or driving a car, sailing relies on certain visual and physical feedback systems. You can experience those only by actually being in a sailboat and dealing with real wind currents.

Now that he had completed his book and learned to put the Klepper together efficiently, Paul was eager to try sailing it. Winter in the Cleveland area lasts well into April, and it was only February. Paul said, "How about going to Deep Creek Lake in Maryland during spring vacation?"

I was less than enthusiastic about the idea and remarked: "We need to buy two life jackets, and why not wait until summer? Or at least find a smaller inlet somewhere."

Paul responded, "You are just too cautious—this will be fun!" We compromised by going to Deep Creek Lake in March as he wanted and buying two safety cushions instead of life jackets. He argued that the cushions were a lot cheaper than life jackets.

When Paul and I and the bags holding the Klepper arrived at the Deep Creek Resort, the temperature hovered between freezing and the low 40s. Next day was boat-launch day, and after breakfast Paul spent the necessary hour and a half or more it took to reassemble the Klepper.

It was cold enough for us to wear heavy jackets, and there were threatening clouds in the sky. But we both ignored them as we pushed the Klepper into the lake, hopped in, and raised both sails all the way. That made the boat top-heavy and very difficult to handle. Paul, using the knowledge he had gained from his book, maneuvered the boat out into the middle of Deep Creek Lake and was delighted to be sailing. We noticed we had the whole lake to ourselves.

Suddenly, the wind shifted, and the Klepper heeled dangerously close to the surface of the water. Paul hollered to me to take down the sails. But before I could do so, another big wind gust hit us, and the boat turned all the way over. The sails caught on the surface of the lake, and we were suddenly plunged into extremely cold water. The paddles and the safety cushions immediately floated out of reach. We clung to the side of the Klepper and realized we were in very serious trouble. Paul suggested, "Maybe we can set the boat back up." We tried to do that, but by now the sails were wet and heavy. The lines seemed to be tangled around everything, including me.

As I struggled to free the sails, I became so entangled in the lines that I was pulled under water, then under the boat. I was convinced I was going to drown right then. Paul dove down, untangled the lines, and pulled me back to the surface. By now we were both completely terrified and out of ideas about what to do. It was too far to the shore to swim, and we were getting colder by the minute. All we could do was cling to the side of the Klepper.

After what seemed like an eternity, but probably was closer to ten or fifteen minutes, an extremely angry man piloting a motorboat appeared around the side of the capsized Klepper.

"You two have got to be the stupidest, dumbest people on the face of the earth," he sputtered as he pulled us to safety in his boat and tied our boat to his.

"Don't you have any sense at all? Nobody takes a sail-boat out this early in the season. You are just very lucky I had my boat on the slip or you would have drowned. And if anybody deserved it—you two ninnies do. What a dumb stunt! Do you know anything at all about sailing? And by the way, you have way too much sail for the size and shape of your boat."

I was so cold my teeth were chattering. Paul, for once, was too abashed to admit he had learned to sail from a book, so we just sat in the stern of the man's powerful mo-torboat and thanked him over and over for saving us.

The man—he never did tell us his name—told us in no uncertain terms to stay out of our ridiculous excuse for a sailboat until we learned how to handle it properly. He also strongly suggested we take a trip to the local emergency room because we were good candidates for pneumonia.

We put on dry clothes. At the local hospital emergency room, the doctors and nurses also told us we were crazy and lucky to be alive. Armed with antibiotics and cough suppressants, we drove back to our rented cabin and spent the rest of the weekend sipping brandy in front of the fire and nursing the bad colds we both developed after our ad-venture.

I tried to say "I told you so," but Paul just retorted, "Shut up, Sheila."

MY CATHEDRAL

Christine Sunda

Here I sit close to the top of the world. Behind me lies the arduous hike up the mountain. Spread out in front like a vision is the Piedmont of Virginia.

Today is clear and humidity-free, unusual for our area. I can see vast distances. Is that faraway smudge Warrenton, Gainesville, or even Manassas? Below me glide elegant and silent vultures, caught in updrafts that flow up the mountainside. The solid rock under me is warm from sun, and crisp air soothes my hot, red face. I'm still panting from the last scramble up the trail before arriving at this piece of Virginia nirvana. I breathe in cool air deeply and listen to the quiet.

I stand up and walk to the other side of the ledge to see more views. Here the parade of mountains stretches ever northward in undulating patterns with deep shadows where valleys lie. Trees march up the sides of the mountains and provide homes for so many animals. Sun glistens off something in the distance, a rock maybe? Above and to my left is more of the mountain remaining to clamber and climb. It will test my endurance, but the end offers strong, cooling breezes.

Here comes the fun part of the hike: climbing rocks shaped like large hammers and squeezing through small rock valleys carved eons ago by wind and water. I love the capricious way these tremendously large rocks are piled one on top the other. It is a wonderful place, an example of nature's magic. After I come around a rock corner, the world again opens up in front of me. The vast plains that stretch out below are slightly smudged with pollution. My eyes, accustomed to focusing on things close up, revel at the distances.

The summit is now here. I think I'm dead, done in by the mountain! I lie on my back with the sun on my face. I hear my loved ones laughing, as they climb on the rock sentinels nearby. Maybe I'll survive after all, though the view is enough to have died for. All these glorious mountains surround me; they are so wise and steadfast. As I drink in the visions around me, they feed my soul. Soon, it will be time to start down the mountain and the long trek home.

Life is good when we have places like this to worship in.

HOMES

Sheila School

I like to watch a program about first-time homebuyers on television. Seeing newlywed couples who are so picky about things like wallpaper and granite kitchen counters set me thinking about the Sixties when Paul and I were first married. What a difference fifty plus years makes in young people's aspirations about housing!

First, we were married for more than twenty years before we finally bought a house. It took us that long to save up a sizable down payment and find a house Paul thought was a good buy. Before then, we rented our homes.

Second, in the Cleveland, Ohio, area where we lived in the Sixties, rental or for-sale houses did not normally come equipped with appliances like washing machines, refrigerators, dryers, stoves, and dishwashers. Gradually, we acquired used versions of most appliances, which made moving even more hazardous. We moved often. You have not lived until you help move a full-sized refrigerator down two flights of stairs and into a rented moving van. We even owned a portable dishwasher—the kind we had to hook up to the kitchen-sink faucet every time it was used.

We bought two heavy, room air conditioners, as central air was not common in our early homes. When we looked at houses, we usually expected to find only one bathroom. Houses had bedrooms—not master suites. We certainly did not quibble about the bathroom décor and were truly grateful if the one bathroom included a shower. The tile universally used in bathrooms in the Cleveland area was small black-and-white, often chipped, and the grout between the tiles was hard to clean. We decorated our black-and-white bathrooms with colorful curtains and towels. We redid the tile only if it was broken and painted the walls only if they were stained.

When I think of our first rental home in Lakewood, Ohio, in 1963 and compare it with the 2010 versions shown to current young couples, I have to laugh. Our first home was the bottom floor of a former single-family dwelling. On the second floor were a small apartment and two individual rental rooms that shared a bathroom. The original house had been a quite beautiful, single-family home with dark woodwork and Tiffany-style lights that had been converted from gas to electricity. Our floor consisted of a large bedroom, a bathroom, a basic kitchen, and a dining room/living room combination. We also had use of a car-and-a-half style garage.

I did the laundry in a wringer washing machine in the unfinished basement. I ran the wash through the wringer two or more times to get it clean and rinsed. I then hung the wash on a clothesline and tried to dry it before the rain came in spring and summer or the clothes froze in Cleveland winters. This hard work consumed most of my Saturdays.

There were wood floors throughout the house, but such floors were not popular. So we saved our money and put down gold, pure-wool carpeting. Our furnishings consisted of mismatched chairs, tables, a couch, and a nice maple dining-room table and chair set. Our bed was a double mattress and frame set, and we had non-matching chests of drawers. The bedroom closet was small and narrow. We had never heard of a walk-in closet, another "must-have" for today's house hunters.

Paul decided the one-and-a-half-car-sized garage was just big enough for both cars, a definite plus in often-snowy Cleveland. However, the garage had no room to spare, and the cars had to be driven into it at just the right angle. This process worked pretty well for a couple of months. But one day I miscalculated and parked the Sprite too close to the garage wall. Paul had already left for work. When I tried to back the Sprite out of the garage, it got stuck against the wall, and I couldn't move it. I stood in the driveway, crying. The man next door took pity on me and pushed the car over and then out of the garage so I could leave for my teaching job. After that, Paul and the Volkswagen had the garage all to themselves.

Paul tended to be a fix-it-your-self-er and a creative problem solver. One hot June day, I arrived home from school to find him sitting in his underwear, reading a text-book in front of the refrigerator. Between him and the open freezer of our fridge was a kitchen chair with a stack of books piled in the seat. On top the books was a camping cooler filled with the contents of the freezer. On top the cooler was an old-fashioned, rotating electric fan turned on full blast. I asked Paul what on earth he was doing. He replied that he was simultaneously defrosting the freezer and air conditioning himself and our kitchen.

An exciting aspect of living in this house was the behavior of the people who lived above us. It was an often-changing group, and we never knew what was going to happen next. When we first moved in, one room was occupied by a woman who vocalized loudly, "Get out of my room, get out of my room," at all hours of night and day. As she was the only one there, she ended up in the local psych ward.

And another woman, who proved to have a nice little night-time business, replaced her.

Our bedroom was right under the new tenant's room and the front stairs leading to the second floor. A scenario with music and footsteps was repeated two or three times a night, especially on weekends. First, we noticed that she played the same record many times a night. "Tonight " was the song that wafted down the stairs. Then, we would hear footsteps going up the staircase and a couple more repeats of "Tonight." Sometime later, we would hear heavy foot-steps going down the stairs. We reported the pattern to our landlord, and he told that tenant to take her record player and business elsewhere.

Eventually, two Native American young men who at-tended an intern program run by the U.S. government rented the small apartment. As it turned out, they were fresh off the reservation and had never lived in a house with a modern stove and bathroom. Several times they turned water on in the upstairs bathtub but forgot to turn it off, and water from their tub leaked through the ceiling onto our new wool carpeting. Even more worrisome was their habit of turning on the gas in their oven and then waiting about thirty minutes to light it. We lived in fear they would blow up the house, themselves, and us at any time. Techni-cally inclined Paul had a talk with them, and they finally grasped the danger of the practice. We thought we had solved all the problems. We had not yet experienced the fi-nal Indian uprising!

At about one o'clock in the morning on a chilly October Saturday night, we were awakened by a loud crash right outside our bedroom window. When we looked out the window, we saw the Indians' pickup truck smashed against a large tree on the lawn. Struggling out of the truck were our upstairs neighbors, drunker than sin. Just fitting their key into the front door lock took several tries, and then they could barely navigate through the doorway. Once in, they had to climb the long back staircase to get to the second floor. On the way up, one of them fell down and hit a beautiful glass lamp at the bottom. We were treated to the sound of breaking glass.

At that point, Paul decided that maybe they were hurt and went quickly to the staircase to see if he could help. One guy was bleeding profusely from a cut hand but would not let Paul anywhere near him. Disgusted, Paul came back and called the police. The Lakewood police took the Indians away, and that was the end of their time in the small apartment.

After that night, we decided we would be better off in a single-family home. We found a dirt-cheap rental in a neighborhood that was being destroyed to make way for a new freeway. That house and the unnerving destruction that took place around it are another story for another time. I will say only that the tale involves pigeons and stucco.

Drawing by Alexandra Mooney

BAT

Jimmy Porter

Booze often keeps people sane during insane times. Perhaps it was booze that kept me sane while in an Army
Special Forces camp in the Mekong Delta of South Vietnam.

In peacetime, living in the comparative luxury of a fort,
the army was a much different place than it was during war.
At the fort, officers used enlisted men to do the most mundane and foolish things. Such tasks included picking up
trash, shoveling manure, digging ditches, and just about
anything you can think of that was strenuous and/or de-

meaning. This sort of treatment ended when an enlisted man attained the rank of sergeant. Being a sergeant was pretty much like being a walking boss on an antebellum plantation in Georgia. You didn't have to do the hard work. You simply carried out the orders of "the man," and thus were hated by both the man and other slaves alike. At our camp in Tan Phu, where Americans were regarded as the enemy, everything changed in 1963.

We respected everyone, even those we hated. The lieutenant and captain may still have thought you were a piece of dung, but you may have been the piece of dung that saved his sorry ass because the Vietcong (VC) would much rather waste an officer than an enlisted man.

Daily life consisted of either preparing to defend the camp against attack or training our strikers—Vietnamese who volunteered to fight with American-Special-Forces—techniques for being more effective in combat. At night, we set ambushes around the camp that usually consisted of a dozen strikers and a couple of Americans. Most of the time the ambushes would have no contact. But occasionally there would be huge firefights when we would call in our "friends." True, we were isolated, but we had friends who could get to the camp very quickly when the proverbial shit hit the fan.

We could call for an air strike. At the time, the aircraft were mostly World War II and Korean War prop fighters. For us on the ground, those aircraft were much better because they flew slower. Pilots could more easily hit targets at 200 mph than they could at 500 mph—the approximate speed of a jet fighter. Of course, it was easier for the VC to hit them at 200 mph, but that was a risk those of us on the ground were willing to take.

Despite protection from above, so to speak, life was lonely. We were volunteers. Yet, we all felt that nobody, save our immediate families, really cared that we were risking our lives for our country. We were in the middle of nowhere, while just about anyone who wanted—man, woman, or child—shot or threw grenades at us. But such things were never spoken of. Perhaps it was because we were supposed to be "tough" Green Berets, or maybe it was a male thing. But the underlying question was never articulated: "What the hell am I doing here?"

There were quiet nights when I felt I would burst with loneliness. Several of us would quietly let the Ba Moi Ba beer exchange reality for wings. In those moments, I was a hero, loved and respected by all. Girls waited anxiously back home to love me when I returned. We would drink and share those "safe" thoughts. In other words, they were mostly total bullshit. By the time someone was drunk enough to say something meaningful, he was too incoherent to be understood. Such gatherings normally did not include the team leader, the captain, or the executive officer, the lieutenant. Our leaders had to maintain a healthy distance between themselves and their charges.

One such night when we seemed to be getting exceptionally soused, I started talking about a girlfriend, and everyone really perked up. Normally, no one would have discussed such a thing. It presented too many paths back to reality. But, since I was nineteen and the youngest one on the team, my companions could listen and comment in the safety of knowing they were worldly wise and above the longing I felt.

For whatever reason, Lieutenant Rick and Captain Gomez joined us. The gathering had the feel of an all-boy, junior high school party where someone had snuck in booze. Imagined and exaggerated stories of sexual conquests poured out, and all twelve of us—the whole team—were discussing life as if we really cared. After a while, when suddenly we noticed a single bat flying above us like a devil or maybe a guardian angel, the conversation began to fray like a cheap pair of pants. The thatched roof of our camp building was a haven for bats. Nightly they chased the abundant supply of insects. Bats, though somewhat creepy, were really protectors. The diseases we could catch from the tons of insects they ate were a lot more sinister than any bat.

The bat moved so slowly, so nonchalantly, and seemingly aimlessly as he weaved against the darkened sky. He seemed so free. I guess he didn't know there was a war going on, at least not yet. Then, from out of the blue, Williams, a demolitionist, fired a round at him from his .45. We were stunned at first, but laughter quickly followed as the bat continued to fly nonchalantly. Williams was kind of a maniac. I guess he thought we were laughing at him, so he quickly fired the remaining seven rounds in his clip, all to no avail. At first he was really pissed, but seeing the continued flapping of the bat above us as though nothing had happened reversed his scowl to laughter.

Then Colby drew his .45 with the announcement, "Let me show you how it's done." After the weapons expert's eight rounds flew safely toward heaven, the laughter became uproarious. Williams laughed so hard that Ba Moi Ba ran from his nose as the bat continued his freedom dance. We all now realized first-hand how good bat radar is, though we were way too far in the bag to touch this creature.

It was the first time I felt truly close to this group of strangers, who had been thrown together to make the world safe for democracy. As I watched their smiles and laughter, I didn't feel the loneliness or anger that had inundated me the past four months.

Without anyone noticing, Sharkey—the team operations sergeant—had picked up his M2 carbine, a fully automatic rifle capable of firing about 700 rounds a minute. Sharkey was a World War II and Korean War veteran and possibly the meanest man alive. He expended a thirty-round clip within a heartbeat as the bat continued his pattern. Our laughter became uncontrollable. But instead of laughing, Sharkey loaded another clip with a sneer. He held back on the trigger until the bat was splattered across the now-mirthless sky. Time ceased.

We stood looking at the noble, now-lifeless, torn flesh. Sharkey's sneer emptied like the last drops of Ba Moi Ba— warm, flat, unsatisfying—his eyes, our hearts uttering, "Damn." "Damn."

DUSK, SEPTEMBER 23, 1968

Bruce Edgerly Roemmelt

It is dusk. In the South China Sea, the USS *Intrepid* is launching and recovering twenty-four A-4 Sky Hawks and support aircraft every ninety minutes all day and all night. The converted anti-submarine aircraft carrier is about one hundred miles from Vietnam. We sometimes call ourselves members of the Tonkin Gulf Yacht Club. I've never been in a yacht club, but I have an idea that this is not quite what it is like.

These hour-and-a-half cycles go on for about ten days until it is time to get more bombs, gas, and chow. Then, we stop flying for a day and go through "Un-Rep," underway replenishment. Next, we sail to a big supply ship that has all the supplies we need to continue our little part of the war effort. Then, back to work. We stay out for about thirty days at a time.

Every thirty days or so, we return to the Philippines for about a week. We do some hardcore partying in Olongopo City outside of the naval base at Subic Bay. Additional repairs and replenishment are done there too. Not much time to develop relationships is allowed. It is not long before we are back at sea, flying missions again.

The ship turns constantly, and we lose our sense of direction. "Airdales," the folks who deal with the planes and flight operations, are less intent on the "real" Navy. I can tell which way we are going only at sunrise and sunset. The most beautiful sunrises and sunsets I've ever seen have been from the deck of that carrier.

The work is hard for the entire crew. Twelve hours on, twelve hours off. Sleeping is tough, as our berthing compartment is fourteen feet under the starboard catapult. You can imagine the noise generated by all that equipment in the process of throwing a big jet plane into the air, one that carries nine 500-pound bombs. Sometimes, it is tough getting rest. Then, there is the odor that develops in a room that can't be more than fifty-by-fifty feet and contains 115 "swabbies."

Steam upwind, launch, and recover; steam downwind, prepare to launch, and recover. Do it again. Most of the real work goes on out of sight of the glamour and excitement of the launches and landings.

Why are we here? I am truly unclear as to our mission. Why am I here? I guess some sense of duty. There is a lot of anti-war activity back home, and some of it is creeping into our lives here. We all wonder why we don't bomb Hanoi, though. What is going on in a war in which there are places out of bounds and off limits? Many of us have a real detached sense of the war. I guess I am ignorant of the political realities. I do know that in America there is a democratic system, and to keep it and change it you *must* pay your dues. My father did in World War II. My country called and I answered.

I am an ABH 3, Aviation Boatswains Mate Third Class Petty Officer (E-4). I am assigned to the crash crew. We provide fire suppression and rescue on the flight deck. When the birds crash, we make sure the fires are out and the pilot and crews are evacuated. We know each plane and how they operate. We are also responsible for some of the things necessary for putting the flight deck in a position to land planes after a crash.

We have a big crane and forklift that can literally dump damaged aircraft into the ocean, if necessary. We have twenty-foot square, one-inch-thick steel plates that we can weld to the deck to cover major holes. I alternate between those jobs. Tonight I am responsible for fire control. In addition to using the high-tech, light-water and purple-K extinguishers, we also coordinate each of the hose crews who apply the ship's water foam and high-pressure sprays. Just like the war, high-tech, low-tech.

The flight deck is a blaze of color, sound, and fury during flight operations. Different crews wear different colored shirts to distinguish their assignments. The crash crew and bomb guys wear red shirts, flight directors and crew leaders wear yellow shirts, and repair guys and plane handlers wear blue shirts. The guys who handle the catapults and arresting gear wear green, as well as the folks who fuel the birds.

The activity is intense, and you have got to keep your head out of your butt or you can get a real thrill being blown down the deck, and maybe over the edge, dropping eighty feet into the ocean

The noise of the jets is numbing. The heat of the exhausts is searing. Intakes on the jets are deadly. Each time they land, they go to one hundred percent power just in case they miss one of the five arresting gear cables. If they "bolter," their power lifts them nicely into the air so they can try again. You have to be careful up here on the deck.

Occasionally, a plane will "crunch" during landing and break something—a main gear, a nose wheel, or something else. "Hung bombs" often release upon landing, bounce on the deck, and splash harmlessly into the ocean. They tell us the detonators need a couple of hundred feet to arm, and we are much too close to the ocean for them to explode. Even though they don't explode, it is a pretty awesome sight to see them bounce and splash!

I once saw a Sidewinder missile fire upon touchdown from an F-8 Crusader fighter. That will make your butt cheeks pucker. I consider the eighty-foot drop into the ocean, should it be necessary. The USS *Forrestal* just had a major fire, and dozens were killed. Our ship is much smaller, and there is less room to run and hide.

Sometimes, the birds are shot up. They can lose hydraulic power and are real sloppy to handle using auxiliary control. Bullets make all kinds of things leak in a plane, especially the pilots. Besides hydraulic fluid, leaking jet fuel is a real problem. From a fire fighter's perspective, it is nice to have the ship turn into the wind. When you are fighting a fire, it is always good to have the wind at your back.

The days and nights are filled with ninety-nine percent routine hard work. As dusk approaches this evening, the 23rd of September 1968, word comes down from the "Air Boss" that a damaged Sky Hawk is coming back and will be landing in the next recovery effort. He was shot up by ground fire over some target, somewhere. There is more tension now. We can see only the light on the wing as the bird comes in on final approach. He needs to land real bad. We assume the pilot is shot and hurt too.

The light on the wing is a real point of focus for those of us watching this plane land. It is an indication of the angle of attack (AOA) of the approaching airplane—the angle it needs to be at to be slow enough to land and fast enough to stay in the air. We have seen thousands of those lights. At dusk and at night, all you can see is that light until the plane hits the deck. This time, the light indicates that the bird is in trouble. All eyes are on those lights for the thirty seconds of final approach.

The nose is going up and down on the injured Skyhawk. We can tell by the lights on the wing. Three lights: red, green, and yellow. Each gives a visual indication of AOA. Red, green, then yellow. Yellow, green, then red. Too fast, too slow. Too slow, too fast. And just before touchdown, way too slow. The Sky Hawk gives up the will to fly, makes a left turn, and crashes into the flight deck and the Landing

Signal Officer's (LSO) platform, then lurches in slow motion into the ocean.

There is a big explosion as the Sky Hawk hits the water. The sea temperature is about 65 degrees, and the hot parts of the Sky Hawk are several hundred degrees. There is a big steam cloud from the port side of the boat. *No fire!* There are several planes in the air that need to land. Fuel is critical, and the birds have nowhere else to go. They have got to land or crash. The pilots either land on the *Intrepid* or pull those yellow and black striped handles and "punch out" (eject). We have to make the flight deck ready for landing. Perform. Do your job. Two dead, one dying, one badly injured.

We get the deck ready to accept aircraft. The injured and dead are evacuated. Emergency landing lights are rigged to guide the rest of the planes in. We bring the birds down after much hectic but organized activity. All the training and discipline pay off. The system works for the pilots in the air. The system does not work for my friend Bobby Lee Spencer, the enlisted radioman for the LSO.

Bobby Lee Spencer is dying, his left leg and right arm ripped from his body by the A-4 as it tumbled across the deck and cart-wheeled into the sea. A terrible wound runs from his left groin to his right chest. The Corpsman apply trauma dressings to Bobby, and we put him in a Stokes Litter. He goes rapidly to the ship's operating room ten decks below. He never had a chance.

Twenty-four hours later, at dusk on the 24th of September 1968, between one of the innumerable ninety-minute, flight-operations cycles, a small memorial ceremony is held. Three wreaths are thrown into the South China Sea to honor the three who died in the crash: the pilot of the plane that crashed, another young pilot who was just observing on the LSO's platform, and Bobby Lee Spencer. A prayer is said. Taps are played. Few tears. Flight Ops in five minutes. No time for pain.

I visit Bobby's name on the Vietnam Veterans Memorial Wall every September 23rd. I think of his sacrifice and that of my 59,000 brothers and sisters whose names are on that wall. I wonder if anyone else thinks of Bobby these days. His death hurts more now than it did at dusk, the 23rd of September 1968. Now, I have the time to hurt.

I FELT THE HEAT

Bruce Edgerly Roemmelt

Each year I make a trip to the Vietnam Veterans Memorial to remember a friend of mine who died in 1968. I make the trip at dusk on the 23rd of September and place the short essay I have included with this letter in a picture frame at the base of Panel 42 W. Bobby Lee Spencer is the first name on the second line.

This year, and every year since this incredible tribute to those who made the ultimate sacrifice was opened, I learned a little more. I learned more about myself, the Wall, and life. There has been much healing at this great monument.

Have you ever had a cut or a bruise? When it is healing, it gets warm. There is probably some simple medical explanation for this, but the fact is it gets warm. I guess the body is sending a message that things are going to be better.

Last night when approaching the Wall with my closest friend Beth, I noticed, for the first time there was heat coming off the marble. I could feel it. It was like a warm wave that washed over me. I stopped in my tracks and said to Beth, "Do you feel the heat?" She answered, "Yes."

In fact, the first time she visited, it was a typical clear twenty-degree cold winter day, and she said she felt the heat right away. Last night was cool and a typical early fall day. I felt the heat.

I started to think about the heat and what it meant. My first thought was I am healing. The Wall is healing, those who served are healing, and perhaps most important, those who lost loved-ones are healing. The work of the Friends of the Vietnam Memorial, the volunteers, and the Park Service are helping, but the Wall is the thing. So I had another reason for this monument in my mind to be felt as a living thing. Sort of like a big marble nurse.

After I placed the remembrance, I sat on a bench with Beth and watched as folks on the walk stopped to read about Bobby. I healed some more.

23 September 1993

VISITING VIETNAM IN 1973

Christine Sunda

My father, a former CIA agent, was stationed in Qui Nhon (pronounced Quin-yong), Vietnam from 1971 to 1973. To be closer to him, my mother and I moved to Taipei, Taiwan. We were known as safe-haven families and lived in special housing. Every six weeks, my father spent seven days with us. This extended his tour by six months but reduced stress on the family. I attended Taipei American School. When I graduated from high school there in 1973, my parents gave me a trip through Southeast Asia.

I began the trip by flying to Saigon to meet my father. Saigon frightened me. I was warned during dinner the first night that motorcyclists had been known to throw bombs into restaurants where Westerners ate. After Saigon my father and I flew to Qui Nhon, which is on the coast north of Nha Trang. American troops had pulled out a couple of months before we arrived. When asked, the people I met there said they thought everything would be quiet in Vietnam for a couple of years. They said America would forget about the country, and the Vietcong would take over. Therefore, I don't know why we were caught so unprepared when Vietnam fell in 1975. The U.S. government had promised many Vietnamese collaborators that they would be evacuated to America at the end of the war. But few managed to leave the country.

Because I couldn't go out without an escort, I spent a month in the CIA compound in Qui Nhon. I stayed there two weeks longer than planned because we were waiting for a New Zealand cargo plane with supplies for a local hospital to arrive and give us a free lift to Singapore. The most striking thing about the compound was the water. The water in Taipei wasn't potable, so I was used to water I couldn't drink. But the water in the Qui Nhon shower was so rusty it stained clothes red! It also had a malodorous smell.

During my visit, we went on a few outings. One was a trip to the "shooting range," a garbage dump where we used tin cans for target practice. I tried out the various weapons issued to agents in Vietnam. The M-16, which was widely used there, got so warm in the tropical heat it became too hot to hold. On our way home, we stopped to get gas, and an eight-year-old girl came begging with a lost and bewildered look in her eyes that no child should ever have. My Vietnamese escort said she was both an orphan and a refugee. Even though I was a self-centered eighteen-year-old ready to go off to college, I wanted to take her home with me—to see that look erased from her eyes.

On another outing, I drove with my father and an American CIA friend from Qui Nhon to Nha Trang, a four-hour trip along the Vietnamese coast. We could travel freely—though for extra protection our friend was riding shotgun with a Swedish K—because my father knew the Vietcong had orders to avoid shooting Americans. He said we were being observed, especially when we slowed for poor roads and bridges, but not to worry. I wonder if my mother would have said, "What do you mean—not worry!"

On the trip we passed through one valley where many thousands of American soldiers had died in during the Tet offensive earlier that spring. The valley was deserted and seemed very strange. I thought I could almost feel the spirits of the dead. Agent Orange had been used to clear the area, but tropical plants had already grown tall enough to cover deserted metal Quonset buildings. Then, a little later, we rounded a corner and came across a breathtaking view of ocean and deserted beaches, huts, and palm trees. It was one of the most beautiful places I've ever seen. It's no wonder Vietnam was once known as the Riviera of the East.

On a third occasion, I rode in a helicopter that was flying reconnaissance over a wide area. I saw hills covered in lush vegetation. I always wondered what information the Vietnamese who ran out to meet us at our various stops passed to the pilot. It was the only time I've been in a helicopter—the same type I saw last year in the Smithsonian.

Sometime later I literally rode shotgun when we drove to a Montagnard village. The Montagnards, aborigines in the Central Highlands of Vietnam, sided with the Americans during the war.

When we drove into the village, it seemed as if we had been transported to an American Indian reservation. The young man I first spotted looked just like a Native American with bright red clothes and a papoose strapped to his back. Apparently, Native Americans and aborigine Vietnamese are related. Both were driven out of central Asia by invaders.

The women in the village we visited wore no clothing above the waist. Now, before being titillated, imagine seeing not only topless young women, but also topless grannies and aunties. After a short while, it didn't seem so strange. Everyone was nice and friendly. I bought a bow, arrows, and native costumes from the villagers. After Vietnam fell, the Montagnards suffered greatly because they had sided with the Americans.

Many of the beaches in Qui Nhon were polluted. However, we could swim at a nice beach outside of town that was part of the local leper colony. I never saw any of the patients. However, I do remember the line of jellyfish called "men of war" that you had to swim through to get into the water.

A group of nurses and doctors from New Zealand operated the local hospital. They gave me a tour of the facility. Even though they had warned me about the conditions, I was shocked to see the overcrowding. At least two children occupied each crib. A gurney covered with a white sheet over what looked like a body stood in the hall. The nurses told me many of them got burned out. They would fight to save the life of patient, but because of a lack of personnel, the patient would die when they went off duty.

When the New Zealand cargo plane finally arrived, my father and I flew to Singapore. The plane's cockpit was above the main part of the plane. With that arrangement, the glass nose of the bird could swing open to allow the loading of large vehicles. We, the only passengers, wore headphones to dampen the engine noise, as there was no soundproofing. I lay on pillows spread on the floor of the glass front of the plane. We flew across the length of southern Vietnam, and I watched the beautiful scenery fly by below. Rice paddies made squares and rectangles that looked like a modern, abstract painting by Klee.

I saw Vietnam as a beautiful country caught during a very tragic time. The trip gave me images I'll never forget and some understanding of the effects of war. It was a unique experience and a high-school graduation present like no other.

I originally wrote this piece for a book that was never published. It was a compilation of personal stories written by family members of former CIA agents. It was to be a sequel to the book, Spies' Wives — Stories of CIA Families Abroad *by Karen Chiao and Mariellen O'Brien.*

A JOURNEY WITHOUT MAPS

Wanda Bryant Ruffin

"A sheltered life can be a daring life as well. For all serious daring starts from within."--Eudora Welty

In 1963, when I read *The Ugly American* and wrote a college term paper "America's Declining Prestige in Southeast Asia," little did I know that my life was about to change. I would soon have a personal, painful awareness of this subject. Within a year, I would embark on a journey that would take me from the life of a sheltered Southern belle to that of an activist desperately pleading my cause before the American public, Radio Free Asia, and even the North Vietnamese delegation at the Paris Peace Talks.

In October 1964, I married Jim Ruffin, a tall, handsome Navy pilot, the man of my dreams. A year later, he left for Vietnam to fly Phantom jets off the USS *Enterprise*. We hoped he would return in May, in time for the birth of our first child, but this was not to be. I moved to Montgomery, Alabama, to be near our families. I missed Jim a lot but managed to get through Thanksgiving and Christmas fairly well. In February, I was visited by a Navy Casualty Officer who told me that Jim was missing in action. I concentrated on the lack of information as a sign of hope, and in fact, gave the name Hope to our daughter.

The year, 1966, required much strength. Jim was declared MIA in February, Gwendelyn Hope (called Wende) was born in May. My maternal grandmother died one week later, Jim's twenty-year-old sister died in August. None of these losses was expected. All were tragic events, yet the birth of a healthy, peaceful child was my symbol that life goes on.

Of the nine years that Jim was MIA, the first were the most hopeful, yet my grief was most private. The government advised next of kin to keep quiet. I knew of no others who shared my status. Jackie Kennedy was my role model, and those who knew my situation appeared to admire my "bravery" and stoicism. Time and change in government/military policy brought contact with other Prisoner-of-War/Missing-in-Action (POW/MIA) families. We began organizing and publicizing the POW/MIA plight. I moved to a small apartment, finished my first master's degree, and began working as a speech pathologist at a rehabilitation center. I juggled the schedule of a working, single mother and made speeches on behalf of the POW/MIA effort to all who would listen.

Four POW/MIA wives lived in Montgomery. Three of us lived on the same street, ironically named Sunshine Drive. Our activities and publicity brought mixed blessings, concern, and sympathy from townspeople, but also gossip about our way of life. I led a very pure life in those days, never even holding hands with another man. Therefore, I was hurt and shocked when I heard the gossip about the "black haired whore, a POW/MIA wife who drives a Thunderbird and lives on Sunshine Drive." Obviously, the gossips had combined our three personalities and projected their own desires into the picture. Not only were the men being spat upon for their role in Vietnam, but so were the women who waited for them.

After five years as an MIA wife in what seemed to be an endless war, I felt an intense need to find out about Jim. I wrote letters and sent packages and behaved as if he were a prisoner of war. Wende had been told so much about her father that he seemed to be a real part of her life, but she was beginning to ask difficult questions.

In May 1971, at a Washington, D.C., meeting of the League of Families of POW/MIAs, I realized that most of those families had at least some evidence about their loved ones' fates. Names were being released and letters were coming from POWs. How I longed for anything to confirm my hopes that Jim was alive! My religion had served me well but definitely had been through some changes. My belief in God was quite shaky, but that night in a DC hotel room, I decided to put it to the test. I prayed, "God, if you exist, please let me know if Jim is alive," then I added, "before Christmas." The next morning, I told my roommate, a POW wife, "If there is a God, I am going to get my answer about Jim's fate, and I will get my answer before Christmas."

I returned to work and found on my desk a brochure for a work-related tour to Europe, with stops including Sweden and Paris, both places of strategic importance in attaining information about POWs. Many events unfolded to allow the trip and put me in the right places at the right times. I spoke with Sweden's assistant prime minister, who actually had a file containing letters of inquiry Jim's parents and I had sent to Prime Minister Olaf Palme and also copies of letters the prime minister had sent to North Vietnam on our behalf. In Paris, I was miraculously granted audience with a North Vietnamese delegate. I expressed to the Associated Press and United Press International my high hopes of receiving information about my husband.

The day before Thanksgiving 1971 saw the arrival of a letter from the American Friends Service Committee. It informed me that North Vietnam reported Jim had never been a POW. This was my answer. Because Jim's plane went down off the coast of North Vietnam, he would have been a POW if he had survived. A news release to this effect publicized what appeared to be an impending change of status. When the government failed to make such a status change, my faith in my answer began to waiver. Confiding this to my minister, I was amazed at his response: "You've come this far, why not pray for confirmation?" So I did, and I was reassured in a week's time by a telegram from Sweden's Prime Minister Olaf Palme, who reported that North Vietnam had no record of Jim as a POW.

From that point on, I was a widow. This fact was accepted by friends and family—including Jim's family—although the government made no status changes since its attempts to do so had met with resistance by some families of MIAs.

The next period of my life was a time of many conflicts. I explained to my five-year-old that her father would not return, and her matter-of-fact response was, "I think we need a new daddy." I must have subconsciously agreed with her and got myself into some complicated emotional as well as legal circumstances. I seemed to be torn between opposing factions in all aspects of my life: my identity as waiting wife as opposed to my gratitude to the American Friends Service Committee, whose views about ending the war were increasingly credible. I grew to hate those who played politics with the war as casualties continued to climb.

When the POWs returned in 1973, I had mixed feelings: unreality, envy, and joy. I believed that soon I would hear about Jim's fate. One and one half years later, Jim's status was officially changed to killed in action (KIA), but still no information was released about how he died. I assumed we would never know anything more. I was wrong.

In June 1983, I was again visited by a Navy Casualty Officer with the same serious manner and almost the same speech. This time, I was informed that Jim's remains had been returned from North Vietnam. It was strange to realize that my seventeen-year-old daughter, who sat beside me during this official visit, had been in my womb during the first notification.

What I thought would be no big deal—after all, it was seventeen years later and we were "over our grief"—became an intensely emotional time. With the return of Jim's remains came new information about his death, information the government had had for many years. Another issue was my daughter's grief and the awareness that she and her father had been cheated of the experience of knowing each other, an experience taken for granted by most parents and children.

The burial at Arlington Cemetery and our first visit to the Vietnam Veterans Memorial were emotionally wrenching, yet healing, experiences. Two years later, I moved to the D.C. area and eventually worked with the Friends of the Vietnam Veterans Memorial. This organization allowed me to start In Touch, a locator service that connects families, friends, and fellow veterans of those lost in Vietnam. We also formed Sons and Daughters In Touch, a support and educational service for those whose fathers are listed on the memorial wall. Many of those young adults were the ages their fathers had been when events on the other side of the world forever changed the course of their lives. For years they had not talked about the events, first because of government policy and later because society didn't want to be reminded of that awful period of our history.

If I could start over on my journey, maybe I would change my destination. Maybe I would persuade my husband not to do what he believed was his patriotic duty. And probably, I would make better decisions along the way. But there have been more than a few times when I've known that I was in just the right place at just the right time and that my journey was coinciding with that of a fellow traveler in such a way as to positively affect the lives of many others. This has made it all worthwhile.

WINTER

Bette Hileman

In the Forties, I spent my early childhood in western Massachusetts. There, the winters were tough, but rather than feeling defeated by them, my family defied them. My sister and I delighted in the season, and despite the inconvenience and hard work involved, even my parents seemed to enjoy the cold. Winters were a source of inspiration and wonder to me as a young child and enabled an episode of pure joy as a teenager. Looking through our small-paned colonial windows at snow falling quietly against pale-blue, distant mountains made me almost completely content.

Nearly every year, snow arrived by mid-December and stayed until late March. On Christmas Eve, 1945, when there was no snow, my five-year-old sister was afraid Santa Claus wouldn't reach our house and we wouldn't have any presents.

Because we had a one-hundred-fifty-foot driveway and lived at the bottom of Tannery Hill—a mile-long, steep slope that descended from the village of Blandford—snow presented special challenges. My family couldn't afford to hire someone to plow the driveway, so shoveling was a major project. After storms, my sister and I tried to help my father clear the driveway. In recent decades, New England snows have often been followed by thaws a few days later. But in the Forties and Fifties, winter temperatures rarely climbed much above freezing, and snow accumulated throughout the season.

Photo by Bette Hileman

One exciting aspect of winter was the enormous pile of shoveled snow that built up at the end of the driveway. It became so deep and packed that it was almost solid. One year, my sister and I dug tunnels and a room in the snow bank and pretended we were Eskimos. The enclosure kept us completely hidden and was warm like igloos we had read about in school.

Getting the car up the mile-long steep hill to the grocery store was a challenge in winter. The roads were plowed quickly in rural Massachusetts. But turning the car from the downhill slope of the driveway onto the uphill road and gaining traction was difficult.

In those days, there were no snow tires or four-wheel-drive vehicles. For treacherous roads, chains usually provided a solution. When my father was home, he put them on. But if he was out of town and we needed to go to the grocery store, my mother did the job. She didn't let winter keep her home without a fight.

I remember many times when we headed out the driveway and tried to climb the hilly road. After a few unsuccessful trials, we backed a few feet into the driveway, reluctantly put on chains, and went on our way. Chains worked. But if we drove more than a few miles with them, one link inevitably broke and the broken chain started banging loudly against the wheel well.

The teachers had the same attitude toward winter as my parents. School almost never closed for snow or ice. The six passenger cars that served as buses to bring in children from all over the fifty-three-square mile township generally managed—often with chains—to navigate both gravel and hard-surface roads all winter. Mud, not snow, was what closed school. In early April, when snow melted quickly, the gravel roads in Blandford became a quagmire of deep, impassable mud. Then, we often had a two-week vacation at the time of year when we hated playing outside.

For my sister and me, the greatest pleasures of winter were sledding and skiing. During our early years in Blandford, we used flexible-flyer sleds with metal gliders to travel as far as we could into the hilly, ten-acre field full of Christmas trees behind our house. After school and on weekends on almost every winter day, we trudged up and down the hill repeatedly, trying for fast, long rides.

When we were five and eight, my parents gave us rudimentary wooden skis. They resembled modern cross-country skis but were simple with one strap that went over the front of the boot. To achieve speed, we spent hours packing the trail by climbing the hill with our skis horizontal to the slope. We also tried to find natural pathways through woods that could be used as ski trails. Once, my father helped us create a trail by cutting the brush and branches that obstructed the way.

For Christmas, when we were ten and seven, my parents gave us downhill skis and boots, and our pleasure with the sport expanded greatly. We had leather, state-of-the-art ski boots and metal bindings that immobilized the toe and held the heel in place with a stiff spring around a groove in the boot. The wooden skis had metal edges that allowed us to make sharp turns, and we applied wax to reduce friction.

We now began to ski most weekends at Otis Ridge, an area that opened ten miles away. At first the hill had only a rope tow, a slow way to get up the slope compared with a chair lift. But it was safer than a chair lift and strengthened our arm muscles. On my first day of skiing, the owner of the area taught me how to do snowplow turns. A year later, I learned more elegant techniques at a ski school in Lenox. My sister used the let-fly-downhill method. She shot down the hill, standing nearly erect with her poles in the air. Her daredevil approach worried me, but almost miraculously she was never injured and never hurt other skiers.

At the time, the rate of skiing accidents was high. The bindings, called "bear claws," held the boots so tight to the skis that a miscalculation often caused a broken leg. Modern bindings release the boot quickly and damage to the knee is the most common injury. Nearly every weekend, often late in the day, the ski patrol brought someone with a broken leg down the Otis Ridge hill in a toboggan.

Usually in Blandford, ice-skating was more of a quest than a reality. Before thick ice had a chance to develop on lakes and ponds, snow almost always fell and ruined the surface. But Carol—the one other girl in my grade school class—and I used to spend a lot of time searching through the woods for places where we could skate. In North Blandford, we found a small, marshy pond that froze quickly because it was shallow. Often we shoveled snow off that pond and attempted figure-skating moves there.

In 1956, at age nineteen, I had my most exciting ice-skating experience. That winter there were ten days of frigid weather with no snow before I returned home from college for Christmas vacation. The mile-long lake near my parents' house had frozen with smooth, thick ice. A boyfriend and I drove to the lake and skated there in the moonlight. We were totally alone. The moonlight was almost as bright as a floodlight, revealing the ice and the dark forest surrounding it. I knew this boyfriend well. He was handsome and kind to me, but I often found him a little boring. By now I could skate fast and almost effortlessly. Traversing that lake in the moonlight and hearing the ice rumble while it froze still further were nearly enough to make me overlook his drawbacks and become as passionate about him as the skating.

HICCUPS AND LAUGHTER

Lori Connolly

This morning at work was like most, except for the hiccups—three times already and it was only 11 a.m. Twice they came and twice they went. This time, I thought they were here to stay. My diaphragm hurt so badly, that applying pressure with my fingers was the only relief, temporarily anyway. I had tried every remedy from a tablespoon of sugar to a tablespoon of peanut butter. I even drank water with my head below my knees—nothing worked.

As I wandered out to the reception area to pick up messages, my fingers still applied to my diaphragm, Nickie looked up and asked, "What's wrong?"

I said, "My diaphragm hurts."

Nickie, a mother of two with another on the way, quickly replied: "Go in the ladies room and remove it."

I laughed so hard the hiccups finally stopped. After regaining my composure, I told her, "The god-made one, not man-made."

HOLE-IN-THE-BACK STORIES

Susan Sinclair

My father had an actual hole in his back. It was on the left side about even with his shoulder blade. His milky-white skin puckered there as it tunneled into his body.

Of course, I noticed it when I was very young, and I remember that he would let me try to stick my little finger into it. That hole was totally fascinating for my friends, even more fascinating than the school janitor's missing fingers. And Daddy, of course, made it more exciting by telling us he had gotten that hole when he was shot by an arrow. Not by any old arrow, but an arrow shot by a real Rosebud Sioux Indian.

Daddy was born and raised in Kenmare, North Dakota, where there really were a good number of Indians, and Daddy really did have a pony. He swore that he and Johnny Jackwitz, his best friend, were out riding on the prairie one day when a band of Injuns started chasing them, whooping and carrying on. He and Johnny rode hell-bent for leather back into Kenmare when one Injun shot an arrow that hit him right in the back, but they kept riding right home with folks all along the way shouting, "Good Lord, that boy's got an arrow in him!" And his poor mother almost fainted dead away when she saw him. She rushed him to the doctor, who yanked the arrow out and patched him up. The doctor said my father would just have to make do with the hole and was "damned lucky to be alive, so stop complaining!"

Well, this story left all us kids spellbound every time we heard it, and there just wasn't anyone anywhere with a better one. But as we got older and Daddy got going on the Injun story, we'd hear my mother muttering in the background that he shouldn't be filling our heads with all that foolishness. We didn't want to disbelieve him, but it was hard to ignore her. So finally when he'd start in, we'd all yell, "Oh, Dan, you're just making that up." Then, he'd get all mad and red in the face, sputter and slap his knee and laugh, "No, by God, it's the God's truth. Don't you listen to her!"

I don't remember when he finally gave in and told us the true story of the hole in his back, but to me this new version was every bit as blood curdling as the Injun one. When Daddy was seven years old, he contracted pleurisy. Like pneumonia, pleurisy attacks the lungs. His left lung had filled with fluid, and he was about to die. He remembered terrible pain, not being able to breath, and feeling as if he were drowning. One night, his condition worsened, and his older brother Jim was sent out to get the doctor. When the doctor arrived, he decided that surgery had to be performed immediately, or little Dan would die. Of course, little Dan heard the entire conversation and, worse, the plans for surgery. The doctor decided the best place to operate would be on Dan's mother's sewing table. Dan was weak and unable to fight back. The doctor and the family grabbed him and put him on that sewing table. They tied him down and gave him some strong liquor to drink to sooth him and take off the rough edges, so to speak. The doctor took a knife and cut right into Dan's lung, put a tube in, and drained the fluid into a bucket on the floor. Daddy said he was mighty scared, and it hurt bad, but in a few minutes he could breath again.

So this was the final story. He reverted back to the Injun story, of course, when grandchildren came along. He couldn't resist those eager, innocent faces, looking up at him and begging for the story about his hole. But as the grandchildren got older and wiser, they too yelled at him, "Oh, Dan, you're just making all that up!" I chuckled to myself as I heard them shrieking when he told them the true story of the sewing table and the little boy tied down there. Proof again, I thought, that truth can indeed be worse than fiction.

    *   *   *   *   *   *

Well, Daddy is gone now, no more crazy laughter, no more children gathered around him, eyes big and intent, listening to his fabulous tales. So you can imagine my chagrin, my dismay, my utter amazement when the other day, going through boxes of memorabilia, I just happened to see a yellowed, folded news clipping and opened it. The article read:

Congressman's Son Out of Danger

James H. X's youngest son, Daniel, was rushed to Minot Hospital earlier this week where he was successfully operated on for pleurisy. He remained in the hospital for several days, and the family is happy to have him home and healthy once again.

POETRY

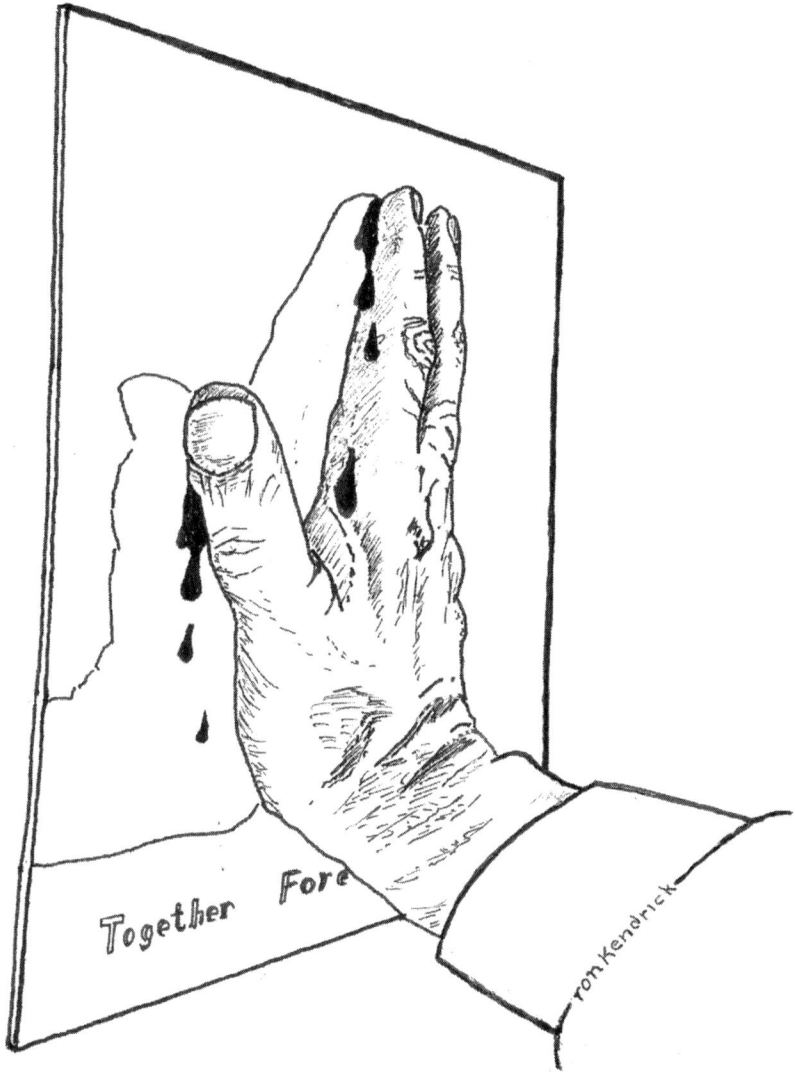

Drawing by Ron Kendrick

A SHADOW OF HER FORMER SELF

Michael J. Crowley

I have scraped; I have painted,
And still her image remains.
She moves from room to room,
As I try to escape her.

When I leave the apartment,
She moves down the hallway beside me.
Her image is on a wall of the elevator.
It moves along the sidewalk,
Keeping up with me as I run.

She is on the windshield of my car,
Transparent enough for me to drive.
I cry, as I have cried so many times before.
I drive to the columbarium,
Where her ashes lie in apparent unrest.

I know you blame me,
But it was not my fault!
I touch her marble plaque
It is cold, freezing.
My fingers stick to it.
I pull violently away.
Blood drips from my fingertips.

She has attached herself to my eyeballs now.
Whichever way I look,
Her semi-transparent image
Hovers in my gaze.
I close my eyes.
I see her clearly
Through the darkness.

Maybe she is right. Maybe I did kill her.
She did not run, when they came.
I swear to you, though, I never wanted them to find her.
She loved me.

I loved her . . .
Maybe . . . Yes, I did love her.
I swear I did.
I was just afraid.
Terrified I would be reported
For harboring one of them.
I should have saved us.

The blood continues
To fall from my hand.
I see her, as I stare at the pool of blood.
I should have saved us.
She was a part of us,
Not one of them.
She was part of the "us" of our love
And the "us" of our humanity.
I sit down and see her image,
As I watch the pool grow.

DIZZY AT BLUE

Michael J. Crowley

I talked with Dizzy Gillespie once,
In one of my past lives,
When jazz and bourbon
Were inhaled
With the surrounding smokes.

Dexter Gordon, Lionel Hampton, Milt Jackson,
Jon Hendricks
Made guest appearances
In that Blues Alley world,
And Stanley Turrentine and Al Jarreau too,
Before they popped out,
When they reached
And soared
And cried
In sound-induced dimensions
Existing akimbo
To our ordinary reality.

In that life
I flew into
Those alternate worlds
With some degree of regularity.
Magic still existed there.

Room.
A small room.
Cloudy.
Separated from Dizzy by feats,
Yet join-linked.
The room itself hurled away,
Smoke, bourbon, and all
Transformed through music's . . .
Through music's . . .
Through music's what?
Power?

No, power is too trivial a word.
Music is not that limited.
Music is not imposed.
It is given,
And playful for all its profundity.

Young I was in that life.
Dizzy was no icon to me.
Neither Beatle nor Stone,
He held no awe.
He just gave me a lift
On that life's road.
He transported me for a while
On that trip.

I once told a coworker
That I thought Dizzy
Should be president.
I will try
Never to curse his name
Like that again.

Between sets, cheeks unpuffed,
He would stand
Toward the back of the room,
Accessible
To his patrons.
Few spoke to him.
Unawed and undaunted,
Well, at least with my daunts
A few sips behind
My physical being,
I approached him.
I let him know
His music brought out in me
Feelings of transcendence.
I groped for the words
To describe the physical
And mental
And emotional sensations,

Which he caused to thrill through me.
He said, "That's soul."

The way he meant it,
I now know,
Was something that comes from
And goes to
The innermost depth
Of personal experience.
What I heard
Was a word
Made trite by catechism class, Soul Train,
And the godfather of soul,
Mr. James "I Feel Good" Brown,
Who, while quite perky,
Decidedly did not induce in me
The spiritual qualities
Of Mr. Gillespie's music,
So I said,
"No, that's not it,"
And went back to my bourbon.

I CRIED FOR THE FATE OF THE WORLD

Michael J. Crowley

"Insanity is just a state of mind."
I told the wooden-legged Indian chief,
Who had just stolen my wallet and my right sock.
"The wolf that howls on Thursday
Brings the moon into alignment with the forest,"
he replied.
"But reality is often relative to consensus," I pleaded.
A passing Buddhist Monk in a green and orange plaid robe
Clapped one hand in agreement, and moved on.
"The Earth is our Mother.
The Sky is our Father.
That Bush over there is our Cousin,
Twice removed on our maternal side."
"Well, I know that holds true
For abstract concepts,
But what we presume to be real
Affects how we act, regardless of objective reality."
The chief got out a sewing kit,
And created a puppet with button eyes from my sock.
It said, "The fire, once lit, consumes
Until nothing remains that it wants."
A snake bit its tail,
And formed a moving infinity sign.
I cried for the fate of the world.
He tucked my wallet into his back pocket,
And merged with the morning mist.

SPIRIT OF LIFE AND LOVE

Rev. Nancy McDonald Ladd

We live in the middle of a mystery,
God's face, if face there be, is veiled,
her voice, if voice there be, is immutable,
and his name, if name there be, is not known in any tongue.

And yet we, here today, seek solace
in the only images we see,
the only voices we hear,
the only names we know
for the mystery that gave us birth.
Here in our unknowing,
may we find comfort and strength in all that surrounds us,
reminders enough in the blessed everyday
of a love that unites us one and all.

We do not know the ultimate name.
We do not see the ultimate face.
But we see one another,
clear as day,
we see ourselves in a community
bound by a mystery.
Even in our own unknowing,
may we be grateful for that gift.

Amen.

Photo by Katherine Mercurio Gotthardt

KITCHEN SCENE

Katherine Mercurio Gotthardt

Thick wrists cinching fingers
by which the slow pestle turns,
the girl tries to grimace away
that old woman poking her piety
at the girl's resistant arm, murmuring
into her still youthful ear,
"You may always be poor,
so you might just as well get good at it, girl."

Still, the girl pounds spice into dust,
black iris eyes tearing at careless fate,
staring into the darkened room,
Away from the table before her:

black bowl of dead fish, rigid with their living eyes,
matching plate of shelled and shiny boiled eggs,
a painting of Jesus and servile women
hanging in front of it all, somehow reflected
in the ancient mirror behind her,
and the little she can add with what she serves
from stone, piling up like sand from an anthill.

Were she of a different class,
she might ask why she has been
sent here. Were she of a different time,
she might rebuke her bonnet.

Had she the constitution and not that
flushed-faced paralysis of the young,
she might just rip the seams of her sackcloth
wrappings and cast them into the bewildered fire,

eyes of the old woman roiling towards the heavens
as she asks what has become of the world.

YOU MADE ME FEEL ILLEGAL

Katherine Mercurio Gotthardt

You made me feel illegal
the way you eyed my hair
too-long-too-dyed-for-work hair
too-third-world-take-care-of-kids hair
too-got-to-clean-the-house hair
too-much-chat-about-the-family hair.

You made me feel illegal
my Walmart pants and blouses
my too-this-isn't-how-we-dress-here clothes
too-cheap-to-even-work-here clothes
too-girly-to-do-your-job-here clothes
too-back-to-the-slum-with-you-dear clothes.

You made me feel illegal
pointing out my jewelry
"too gold" you say, "too gaudy"
my too-don't-show-your-face-in-the-lobby jewelry
too-you-know-nothing-about-our-country jewelry
too-go-home-to-anchor-babies jewelry.

You made me feel illegal
like I'm too-you-can't-speak-like-we-know how
too-got-no-right-to-talk now
too-got-to-go-and-wash-sticky-floors now
too-better-go-cook-in-a-filthy-kitchen now
too-best-sweep-up-the-dirt-you-see now.

You made me feel illegal
too-nothing-more-than-low class
too-nothing-less-than loathed
You made me feel illegal.

You oughta be illegal.

IN SEARCH OF EL DORADO:
A Letter to his Lover

Katherine Mercurio Gotthardt

My Sweet Matilda:

The sun has plopped its heavy body
between two mountains,
while men like me reflect in letters;

we are odd, humans hunching
in near twilight—we write,
yet we cannot leave.

To tell you that I miss you dearly,
that this dark adventure is endless,
that I long to touch the lips I have left

in search of something better, something
brilliant, molten, unusual, would be
to admit my folly. But I have been foolish.

Our search thus far is fruitless—
no gold, nor hint of gold, no
placid kingdom where every stooping
subject picks dusty jewels, no

rivers bearing gifts. Daily we pan
for perfection, yet each screen ends up
empty. How far I have wandered
for nothing.

HOLOCAUST HAIKU

Katherine Mercurio Gotthardt

In the Auschwitz room
four women taking pictures.
Do they scrap-book them?

RESCUE DOG

Sheila School

You look up with Spaniel eyes
That are dark pools of hope
Overlaid with flashes of fear.

With the dignity befitting the progress of royalty,
You permit the stranger to approach.

You are careful—
Yet filled with the joy of a naturally friendly nature.
Your caution is born of experiences only you can remember.
Your small, black, fur-covered body
Is tense with the pain of deciding.

"Are you okay? Will you be my friend?
Should I run, or should I stay?"
The freckles on your nose flash here and there,
And you chance a wiggle or two.
You're a rescue dog—and no one can hurt you now.
You desperately want to believe, but—

In your brief life, you ran wild
Through a sometimes unfriendly world,
Bore and mothered six beautiful puppies—all adopted.

Now you just want to be a dog,
Crawl in your new momma's lap,
And be safe, warm, and not hungry any more.

Welcome to the rest of your life, Lilly.

Lilly, originally called Lillith, was rescued and fostered by the Oldies but Goodies Cocker Spaniel Rescue Group of Northern Virginia. I adopted her in October 2009.

Photo by Alexandra Mooney

DIRTY SALLY

Bette Hileman

The children found a kitten
under the school bus.
She, a six-week-old lump of fur,
had grease stains on her back.
Could they keep her?
We already have a cat, I said.
But I guess so.

The children washed away the stains
and named her Dirty Sally.
She grew up.
She was not good about cleaning her fur.
That was too much trouble.

At ten months, Dirty Sally gave birth to four kittens.
In the beginning, she stayed with her offspring,
leaving them only to eat.
Like all good mothers,
she cleaned the kittens' fur, nursed them,
and slept with them.
But when the kittens were two weeks old,
she started to abandon them.
She was in heat again.
Who would take care of the kittens? we wondered.

No worry. Dirty Sally had help.
The other female, who had been spayed,
stayed with the litter
when Dirty Sally was away.
She licked them and slept with them
and comforted them.
Dirty Sally returned to the kittens only to nurse.
Was she a bad mother?

Published in vox poetica

LEAVE TAKING

Bette Hileman

There was an evening
When you couldn't stop crying.
We were sitting at dinner.
Candles were lit.
The food was delicious.
I was wearing an attractive dress.
The room was quiet.

"Why?" I asked.

"It's all too beautiful.
It won't come again," you said.

"But why?" I repeated.
"I will see you.
There will be other times."

Ten years have passed.
You are no longer part of my life.
Now, I understand
Your tears.

Published in vox poetica

FORGETTING

Bette Hileman

You want to write about him
So you will forget him.

You will not forget the sadness, the craziness.
But the good times, the humorous times,
Will become clear.

As you grow older and lie in bed thinking
Those moments
Will comfort you.

He will appear in your dreams
And your conscious thought
And relieve your loneliness.

You will understand
Why you loved him.

Published in vox poetica

AWAITING SNOW

Bette Hileman

I wake at two a.m.
Everything is still.
The city, waiting with bated breath,
Makes no sound.

At first, I imagine the electricity has gone out.
But the stove clock is lit.

I look at the park through a third-story window.
Not a single branch moves.
The air inside feels different, somehow dismal.
Is it the low pressure
Preceding the storm?

This snowfall may exceed any in history.
Will our power fail?
Will our food and water last?
It is too quiet.
I'm afraid.

Published in vox poetica

Photo by Ginny Ax

DEATH TOO EARLY, TOO LATE

Bette Hileman

The trouble with death is
It comes at the wrong time.
If a friend dies with all his faculties
And in apparent good health,
We say, "It's a tragedy.
He had many good years ahead of him."

If a friend dies in poor health
And for years hasn't been able
To walk, or read, or remember anything,
We say, "It's too bad
She had to suffer.
We don't want to live that long."

Published in vox poetica

Photo by Bette Hileman

MORNING BIRDS

Lily Stejskal

I sleep.
Birds serenade me into wakefulness.
Good morning, Birds.
I love you, too!
Will you always be here for me?

Is this your last springtime here?
Next spring will you pass me by?
Will climate change alter your path too much?
Even if we cannot change back what we've done,
Please birds,
Come see me again!

I AM NOT A CONTRIBUTOR

Lily Stejskal

I am not a contributor.
I do not drive gas-guzzling cars.
I avoid methane products when I can.
I turn off lights when I leave the room,
I turn off my computer at night,
So why does climate change affect me?

Well, I guess I am.
I guess I am a contributor.
My showers are too long.
I always sleep with the light on,
But those are my only mistakes.

Even so, it seems we are trapped.
Even people who care contribute,
Being a polluter is hard to escape.

HUMAN'S CURSE

Lily Stejskal

All humans are polluters,
Whether we want to be or not.
Regardless of our living style,
Beliefs, or love for Earth.
What is the reason?
There may be too many of us,
We may be born with sin.
Whatever the reason,
Environmentalists must fight hard,
For the right to not pollute.

AUTUMN POEMS

Lily Stejskal

Autumn's Entrance

The summer's come and gone.
The rain has sung her song.

She's cleansed the autumn air
Of summer's heat and sweat.
The air is fresh and cool.
Birds splash in puddles and sing.
Insects serenade loudly,
Autumn's as happy as spring!

Autumn Gloom

Autumn is around us.
The skies are grey and rainy.
The leaves no longer green.
All hope, warmth, and freshness is gone.
The warmth of Mary Baldwin,
The freshness of green leaves,
And the hope of spring.

But spring will come again,
And I shall return to Staunton,
To look once more upon
The college where dreams come true.

Mid-Autumn

True Colors
May all leaves show their colors,
The true ones, not the greens,
And may they shine their brightness
Before they turn to brown.

May golden leaves shine brightly,
May red ones' deep glow show,
May orange ones burn like fire,
May yellow ones twinkle like stars.
May all of them sparkle like gemstones,
Before it is time to fall.

Autumn Picnic

Girl hops like rabbit,
With feet in sack she bounces,
On to other side.
Popcorn on my feet,
I gently waddle along,
Like penguin with chick.

Walk with egg on spoon,
I carefully cross the field,
Cluck like chicken, lay!

Pass ball up, under,
Moving slow like turtle,
I'll never win race!

Tip-toe on with spoon,
Foam hands dropping like fall leaves.
I drop them like tree!

Photo by Ginny Ax

GARDENING PRAYERS

Lily Stejskal

Spring is a time for transplanting,
for we all must be transplanted in order to grow.
Let us all be transplanted,
so we can experience the beginnings and renewal of spring.

May Mother Nature bless these plants so they bring us good
food in seasons to come.
We have cared for our Mother Nature.
We have cleansed her of toxins
and offered her these flowers

so she may shine more beautifully than last spring.
Just as we have given Nature these offerings,
may She offer us a productive summer
and a bountiful harvest in months to come.
May She also be our teacher and playmate for all of eternity.

LAMENT AT BRUU FOOD PANTRY

Liz Alcauskas

Spanish as a language is not difficult
Pero para mí, no es fácil.

But I can't remember the nouns and verbs.
No me recuerdo las palabras.

The verbs forms don't quite match ours.
Es importante que usted emplea correctamente el subjuntivo.

People tell me to watch soap operas in Spanish:
Las telenovelas tienen bastante español básico.

We do have a TV, but I have time to watch only the news.
No me gusta mirar la televisión en inglés, ni en español.

Practice speaking is what I need, but I can't do
conversations.
*Hablo español al Food Pantry pero las palabras son también
lo mismo: Cuántas personas hay en su familia? Quiere usted
cebollas? Papas?*

Talking with children is a fine way to have basic
conversation—no discussions of politics or religion.
*Los niños no comprenden que yo no se lo que ellos están
diciendo, pero ellos conversan bastante.*

Is my role to speak Spanish to them?
O, ayudarlos hablar inglés?

*Incorrect translations here illustrate how little Spanish the Americans
know. Their fluency in Spanish is even more limited than the English of the
immigrants.*

SPIRIT SPEAKS

Kathy Sanchez

Spirit speaks, but the voice is her own.
She gives it willingly,
Courageously banishing her ego
To make room for Truth.
She knows not what it will say,
Only that it will speak.

She trusts It with the absolute faith
Of a child jumping into her mother's arms.
Not thinking of herself,
Or worrying about social niceties.
Not caring about what others may say, or think.
She opens to It, feeling no need to judge the message.

Truth isn't always as polite as we'd like it to be.
But it has a message that must be heard.
The message is based on love, of course,
But love isn't always gentle.
Even Machiavelli knew that!

She's not afraid, though;
She's a warrior, after all.
A warrior of the Spirit.
Ever aware that she is part of the Great Mystery,
A living reflection of pure, potent energy.

Sometimes the messages don't make sense,
Even to her.
But she trusts the Messenger,
So she reports them, nonetheless.
For she senses the magnificence in their nonlinearity.
They are Truth. Their essence is pure.
In their perfection, they overcome
The limits of flawed language.

Sure, others may judge her,
Thinking her strange or a bit spacey.
But that doesn't matter to her.
The Great Mystery has asked for her help.
For her, that's reason enough.

ESSAY

Photo by Steve Clapp

TO BE A SIGNPOST

Rev. Nancy McDonald Ladd

John the Baptist was quite a character. This guy, Jesus' friend and mentor, is unique in the culture and mythology of the Christian tradition. You know the image of him— long beard and a great big mound of hair, complete perhaps with some oddly shaped sticks poking out of it here and there, remnant reminders of the fields in which he slept. John the Baptist is remembered kind of like the Grizzly Adams of Jesus' time, chasing around the wilderness wearing a shirt made of camel's hair and eating locusts and honey for dinner. And yet, however strange a figure he may be, standing there with locusts on his breath, there's something about John the Baptist and the work he was called to do that I recognize as a calling for all of us.

In the account of Luke, John is miraculously born to a barren old woman and emerges from the womb talking from his first breath, praising God before he opens his eyes. Eventually, this prodigy of a child grows up to be a preacher, but instead of talking himself up, pretty much the entirety of John's ministry consists of running around telling folks not to get too excited about him. After all, he essentially says, "I ain't the one you're looking for."

In the words Mark gives him, "One mightier that I is coming after me. I am not worthy to stoop and loosen the thongs of his sandals. I have baptized you with water. He will baptize you with the Holy Spirit."

And here's where John starts to feel familiar, not so much in the content of his prophecy as in the nature of it. Not unlike a painter whose masterpiece was never meant to be completed, not unlike a crusader for justice who fights just as long as he has breath for fighting, or a grandmother who goes to her end days knowing that the love she's poured into those children will come to its fruition only in the generations to come. John's whole life, his whole mission, was to be the beginning of something, but not the end of it.

He was destined, from his first words of praise, to start what he could never finish. He existed only to play second fiddle to the future he hoped to help bring about. He was the culmination of nothing, and he lived his whole life knowing that everything he did and said paled in comparison to the future to which his whole life pointed. All he did was point the way. His task was not to be the savior of the world. His task was to be a signpost.

We do not have to be saviors to be enough for the tasks before us. We do not have to mend the rifts in this broken world alone. Sometimes, our task is to call out truth into the wilderness of a painful world, to speak of great things to come and hope with all our hearts that people might dare to believe they are possible. We do not have to prove our worth by fixing it all. All we really have to do is point the way. Like John the Baptist, may it be enough sometimes for us to keep pointing the way, passionate harbingers of things to come, and may we remember that, though the work may not be ours to finish, we are not and never will be free to desist from beginning it.

Photo by Ginny Ax

MANDALA ROUND

Davis Chung

The choir was rehearsing "Mandala Round" at Bull Run Unitarian Universalists church. Mandala is variously translated from Sanskrit as "essence and having" or "containing," as well as "circle-circumference" or "completion." When we began singing the music, my thoughts started drifting to many memories, including watching Tibetan monks create a sand mandala at the Smithsonian's Sackler Gallery soon after September 11, 2001. Just as that sand mandala was a circular image comprised of many smaller images, our vocal mandala was a musical round composed of layers of sacred chants from around the world.

The monks began constructing their mandala by drawing a circle seven feet in diameter. They used long, narrow cones, similar to cake-decorating tools, patiently tapping the narrow ends from which colored sand trickled out, filling in the intricate designs. We started our song with the seemingly simple "Om"—the primal vibration of the universe. Then, we added layers of simple native chants that built an increasingly complex sound. We sang most of the chants in languages for which I have limited comprehension. That lack of understanding reminded me of a recent service at my wife's synagogue.

There, I was fumbling with a book that was half written in Hebrew. The text was unintelligible, and my Western eyes told me the book was printed backward. A chant began, and my frustration grew when I couldn't find the translation. How could I get anything out of the chant if I didn't know the words? Unexpectedly, the women and men started to sing in harmony, and the beauty of the sound shook me from my search for English. I was transfixed by the chant. I felt a warm power course through me as I realized that knowing the words wasn't necessary for me to be moved and to receive a hint of the sacred.

My mind returned to the choir room as our voices added more chants from monotheistic faiths. Even with the broad variety of traditions and languages, the words and tunes blended together, forming a structure that seemed harmonious and complete. In the sand mandala, the many painstakingly added images created a coherent and beautiful picture. This spiritual meshing of chants nudged my mind toward another memory.

Years before I joined this congregation, I was in the BRUU fellowship hall, attending a gospel music workshop led by Ysaye Barnwell of Sweet Honey in the Rock. Many of us from the interfaith gospel group, of which I was a new member, had come to learn from this master. Given my musical background—the Episcopal Church's Royal School of Church Music—I desperately needed the training offered in this workshop.

I had been a bit frustrated by the large amount of repetition in gospel music. Some of this was pride. I thought the sacred music I had learned was more "challenging" and therefore "better." Halfway through the workshop, I realized that gospel music is similar to Hindu chants that are repeated for hours or English plainsong chants of my former church that repeat the same musical line. Gospel music also resembles whirling Dervishes, prayers at the synagogue that usually start with "*Baruch atta Adonai*," bowing towards Mecca five times a day, praying with a rosary, repeating hallelujahs in Handel's "Messiah," endlessly spinning Tibetan prayer wheels, the dancing and singing of First Nation people around a fire or, for that matter, the cycle of the seasons. When we focus on repetition, it thrusts us out of the everyday and the ordinary toward the sacred and the extraordinary. I shared this thought with Ms. Barnwell, and her face glowed with a broad smile as she said, "Yes, yes! You get it!" It was an example of a phrase I would later hear during a sermon at BRUU: There are many different wells, but they all draw from the same spiritual source.

My attention returned to the choir room as the layers of chants in the Mandala Round were pared down until only the Om remained, and I could scarcely contain my tears. Brushes with the sacred do that to me. Then, much as the vibrations of a bell slowly become still, the last Om faded into silence. I often forget that silence is an integral part of music. During this pause—which to me seemed far longer than the few seconds it actually lasted—we had to contain the energy imparted by the song and hold the silence. It was almost too much, and I felt as if I were vibrating. The silence remained until the conductor lowered her arms. Looking around, I saw many smiles around the room.

It is fitting that our song ended with silence because the feelings that engulfed me, fueled my smile, and filled me to the point of bursting went far beyond the scope of words.

MY EXPERIENCE OF THE FEMININE DIVINE

Pat Malarkey

"Surely it is much more generous to forgive and remember, than to forgive and forget." Maria Edgeworth, Irish writer 1767-1849

In 1965, I began first grade at St. Patrick's Parish School in Pottsville, Pennsylvania. Before then, I didn't know there were things I could and couldn't do, things I should and shouldn't do, things I could do now and things I had to put off, simply because I happened to be a girl.

Supervised by the Sisters of St. Joseph, we children lined up twice a day to go to the bathroom. The boys always went first. Not fair! When we had a fire drill, the boys went first. Not fair! I couldn't be on the safety patrol and I couldn't serve on the altar because I was a girl. Not fair!

But the most-not-fairest thing of all was that God was a man—father and son—and the Holy Spirit was a dove. As a girl, how was I supposed to fit into all of this?

Each year of the twelve I spent in diocesan schools, I drifted further away from Catholicism. Junior year in high school, after lots of screaming, yelling, crying, and arguing with my parents, I stopped going to mass.

By the time I got to college, I'd dismissed all organized religions. It seemed to me that they all had the built-in misogyny of father, son, prophet, and so forth. Women were conspicuously absent from the pantheon. Not fair! So I wasn't exactly on the ball when a friend in my dorm told me she was a Unitarian Universalist and tried her elevator speech on me. I filed UU away to think about later.

Photo by Ginny Ax   Heather Hills, Ireland

Later turned out to be the early Nineties. I had just moved to Northern Virginia and was having a horrible time both at work and in my social life. I was spiritually sick and looking for help on the path when I took UU out of my mental filing cabinet for good.

With the assistance of the UU congregations I've called spiritual homes since I moved to this area, I began to find the feminine aspect of the divine. The "Cakes for the Queen of Heaven" class at the Reston UU Church was an eye-opener. I took a workshop, including guided meditation, with Carole Eagleheart. Each step left me more clear-headed, more confident, and more content.

But I was still extremely angry with the Catholic Church, and I knew I'd never be completely happy until I let go of that anger. It was getting in the way, muddying the path I was walking.

In the early 2000s, I decided to face my anger head-on. I began looking for women's tour groups focused on the feminine divine. To my complete surprise, I found one that had a spiritual pilgrimage to Ireland, the land of my ancestors. What better way to push forward than by going back?

So, in 2003, I went on a tour of Ireland with Sacred Journeys for Women. There were twenty-three other women on the tour. Each of us had her own hopes for the trip. I hoped to find what I thought would be the remnants of the "Old Religion" in the very Roman Catholic land of my ancestors. In particular, I wanted to discover the feminine aspect of the Divine and find if She had any resonance for me.

Ireland is a breathtakingly beautiful country, and one of the first things I discovered is that the land itself has human contours larger than life. The ancient Irish did not fail to notice this. Twin mountains in Kerry, called the Paps of Anu today, were called *Dha Chioche Dhanann* in the ancient language, meaning Danu's Two Breasts. Atop each mountain, the ancients constructed tall cairns, clearly visible from a distance—just in case you didn't understand the Irish language, of course.

Many of the places we visited were sacred for the early Christians and, later, Catholics. The Reasc Monastery on the Dingle Peninsula was an early Christian abby. Here, men and women lived and worked together and shared leadership. The director of the monastery was as likely to be an abbess as an abbot.

St. Gobnait's Church in Kerry is no longer in use, but many families bring their daughters there when they come into womanhood. An arch on one side of the church has an ancient Sheila Na Gig as its keystone, and it is thought that a girl on the brink of womanhood will have good luck and prosperity if she touches the Shiela's yoni. Nearby is a fairy mound with Gobnait's well, where visitors come to drink and splash themselves with the healing water. They leave ribbons in thanks to the fairies who keep the water flowing.

Gobnait, herself, was a healer and a beekeeper who left her pagan family to join the early Christian church. She had a dream that she was to build a convent on the site where she saw three white bulls. She followed her dream, and it stands to this day.

My favorite part of the tour was our visit in Killarney with Sister Mary of the Brigantine Order. We started our day with a circle in the convent. A circle in the convent? This was going to be good.

After our circle, the Brigantine Sisters explained their mission to us. St. Bridget was an Irish goddess before she became a saint. While Bridget was a goddess, sisters of her order kept a flame alight for her at the entrance to her temple. After Bridget became a saint, sisters of her order kept a flame alight for her at the entrance to her temple. Recently, the Brigantine Sisters had been given permission to relight that flame, which had been extinguished for hundreds of years.

As a goddess, Bridget had three aspects. Sound familiar? One ruled poetry, writing, and inspiration; another ruled healing, herbology, and midwifery; and the third ruled the fires of the hearth and of the smith and smithery.

As a saint, Bridget became a nun. Sounds like a cop-out, no? Well, the story Sister Mary told us is that, when Bridget took her vows, the archbishop mistakenly read the vows for installing a bishop. And, so, Bridget became the first and only woman bishop of the Catholic Church.

The Brigantine Sisters see Bridget as a bridge between the old and the new. They honor both. And, yes, I was surprised to learn that they are a Catholic order.

We saw many, many other beautiful, sacred places, and time is, unfortunately, too short to describe them and tell their stories today. Some of the women on the tour were disappointed. They felt we went to too many Christian or Catholic places. Ireland is, indeed, full of wells, shrines, and fairy mounds that have nothing to do with Christianity.

But I was thrilled. I learned some valuable lessons on that beautiful green island.

First, true Irish Catholicism is a palimpsest of ancient spirituality overlain with Christianity. The old and new religions coexist and commingle amid the forty shades of green. This is probably because the Romans never had more than a settlement or two on the island. Christianity did not come to Ireland by the sword. Rather, it came in gentle waves from across the Irish Sea.

Second, I began to understand my family members' devotion to Roman Catholicism and its inherent male-dominated theology that excludes all else. In the United States, they had no connection to places like the Paps of Anu, St. Gobnait's or St. Bridget's flame. There was no palimpsest for my father and my mother. I now feel sorry for them because, after only two generations removed from the old sod, they just plain lost half their spiritual selves.

Third, the Irish people are wonderful. They've pulled the wool over the eyes of both the Catholic Church and the British for so long, holding true to their heritage and to their version of Christianity. It's said that a true Irishman—or woman—can tell you to go to hell in such a way that you'll look forward to the trip. There ought to be a medal for that kind of chutzpah.

Last, I finally let go my anger toward the Catholic Church and found the feminine in the divine. They were the goals of my trip, and I had no idea when I set out if I could achieve them or not.

I did not achieve my goals or come to my conclusions as soon as I set foot on the ground in Dublin, nor did I have an "aha!" moment while I was on pilgrimage. It took a long time of thinking, re-reading my journal, e-mailing the friends I'd made, putting together a photo album, and sharing and talking with friends to come to the quiet peace I now have. The work of pilgrimage is done after the return home.

Drawing by Ron Kendrick

UNDER COVER ETIQUETTE

Davis Chung

near miss on a rainy city street provokes this thought. If umbrellas bump, do you say, "Excuse me," as if you had physically collided or do you just keep walking? Having been raised in the country, I am unaware of urban umbrella etiquette. Perhaps I can decipher more proper behavior while walking to the bus.

That close encounter with a pedestrian appears to be a secondary result of one aspect of etiquette: Umbrellas are to be held at an angle that discourages eye contact. While this preserves privacy and prevents spots on glasses, it also decreases the warning time for impending collisions.

I note two other categories of pedestrian. I label them: "Unprepareds," sporting flat hair, speckled glasses, and soggy shoulders; and "Hi-Tech-ers," snug in their Gor-Tex fabric coats. I observe one advantage the latter hold over me with my umbrella. When meeting a loved one, a jacketed pair smoothly performs a greeting and kiss. I watch a couple with umbrellas work through a brief and awkward dance reminiscent of a first kiss with a new date. You remember: on which side does one's nose go? Left? Right? Bonk! Now the question is whose umbrella goes on top of whose? His?

Hers? Bonk! Distance prevented my hearing if either the man or the woman said, "Excuse me."

I observe a woman struggling with her umbrella against the wind. I note the wind direction and take a place upwind to block her from the gusts. Could this be the modern equivalent of laying my cape across the mud over which the lady may walk? Unfortunately, the wind shifts before the woman can notice and thank me for my thoughtfulness.

This raises the issue of high-wind technique. Grasping only the umbrella handle leaves me at a mechanical disadvantage, but I see no one using two hands. Now pride collides with etiquette. Will I appear wimpy? Will others snicker? Curse my testosterone! I am sure women never worry about such issues—one more reason why they outlive men. I go with two hands and hope no one notices. I keep the edge of the umbrella low, hiding my potential shame and continuing the spot-free status of my glasses.

After waiting under a convenient overhang, I see my bus arrive, probably seventy feet away through the rain. That poses my final etiquette/pride question: umbrella up or down? Down, and I look confident and cool; up, and I risk looking wimpy again. I choose up. Why get spots on my glasses? Why have wet clothes for the long trip home? Why am I the only one whose umbrella is up? Oh, I see, it stopped raining.

Slowly I collapse the umbrella and, just to show that it was up for a reason, give it a good shake. Sadly, far from disguising my gaffe, all this accomplishes is to deposit spots on my glasses.

WHO GETS TO NAME GRANDMA?

Carol Covin

"I have a friend who is the second child in her family but had the first grandchildren. She got very upset when her older sister later insisted on letting her child pick names for the grandparents and then demanded that my friend's children change."

New mother

So, who picks? The grandparents? The parents? The children? Is there really a right to the original birth order of the siblings, even if the birth order of the grandchildren is different?

I imagined that I was a very young-looking grandmother when my children both announced they were expecting. Friends flattered me by agreeing. So, the question became if I look and feel too young for the old, wrinkled, stooped, gray-haired, rocking-chaired, knitting image we all assume goes with our culture and our own memories of our grandmothers, then, what should I call myself?

One friend came up with the name "Glam-ma," short for Glamorous Grandmother. I loved it! When I announced to one of my sons that I had found just the right name for my new station, he and his wife were crushed, as I quickly saw by the shocked looks on their faces. Her grandparents had all died before she was old enough to know them and her parents had both died within a year of their marriage. My son stammered, "You will be our child's only grandmother. We thought you'd be honored." Well, of course, I am. And, that settled it. Grandma it is.

Granny Guru's Grains of Wisdom

Names are part of a person's identity. Children can adjust to whatever the decision is—even if each has an individual name for Grandma.

I know of many families who wait until a child mangles the words grandma and grandpa and set the pet name as Gamma, Gammy, Gam Gam, Paw Paw, Gamps or some such version that belongs to the first child who says it and the rest then learn it. It is an affectionate bond between grandparents and grandchildren. One woman told me the first grandchild in her family was dyslexic, so Grandma came out Mugga. The grandmother didn't really like it, but all the grandchildren who came after adopted it.

Others rely on cultural traditions for names: *Nonnee* or *Nonna* (Italian), *Abuela* (Spanish), *Baba* (Serbian), *Bube* (Yiddish), *Lola* (Phillipino). A young grandmother recently told me she is "Baba," because she was always singing "Ba-ba-ba...Ba-barbara Ann" when her grandchildren were visiting.

French-speaking Eleanor Roosevelt asked her grandchildren to call her Grandmère, also the title of a book about her, by her grandson, David. A recent survey suggests Nana is the most common choice, followed by Grandma and Me-Maw.

In my own family, we used Grandma and Grandpa Last Name for two grandparents and Grandma First Name for the third. Grandma First Name, I found out as an adult, was my grandfather's second wife, some years after the death of his first. She never had any children and didn't like the idea of being called grandma. She wanted us to call her by her first name. My mother thought this was disrespectful, so they compromised on Grandma First Name.

Some shorten this convention to Grandma First Letter of First Name, as in Grandma-O. A friend came up with G-Mom, which I think captures her impish spirit. A young woman recently told me her grandmothers were "Rick-Rick" and Other Grandma. Rick-Rick being the closest she could come to pronouncing cigarette. The grandmother of eight-year-old twins told me she is "Grammy." A singer, she says, "This is probably the closest I'll get to a Grammy award."

Another mother told me that in her family the first grandchild was deaf, so signed Grandmother and the next grandchild continued the use of Grandmother. Later grand-children followed the common Southern tradition of Me-maw. Grandma still signs Christmas tags with the appropriate designation. Another grandmother told me recently that she has a blended family, so natural and stepchildren's children have all come up with different names for her.

There are few other relationships where a name is so open to discussion and negotiation as that of what to call the grandparents. It is not a legal designation, but one of love. But, perhaps it is also one of power, as power shifts from one generation to another, or even within generations. Recognizing that power play may help shift the discussion back to love

Children learn quickly that people have more than one name. Adults have one name for each other, another for their children to use, and another more formal name. Relationship names are part of a child's world from the very beginning. They will call their grandmother whatever they are encouraged to—and, she will come whenever her precious grandchildren call.

A SPECIAL TIME

Richard Demaret

I'm not a morning person, not an early bird, nor a morning glory. I don't enjoy getting up early. Yet, I frequently rise before the birds and the sun.

This is a special time. It is a time of quiet, solitude, and peace, a transition between night and day. A time when the owl is finishing its rounds, when night creatures are finishing their tasks, and day critters are getting their last sleep. The moon is up, and the sun not yet risen.

Photo by Bette Hileman

This is a time before the masses of humanity have yet to stir, a time before work and school and before the duties of the day.

It is my time for quiet reading, for making tea, and for updating the computer's anti-virus/anti-malware programs. It is a time to check the coming day's weather forecast. Will it rain or snow today? How hot or cold will it be? When will the sun rise and set?

It is nice to settle back in a comfortable chair with a book and mug of tea. How wonderful it is to read great books, the spiritual mainstays of various traditions—*The Bhagavad Gita*, *The Dhammapada*, *The Yoga Sutras of Patanjali*, and the like! It is wonderful and joyous to learn and reflect upon words and teachings of the great masters. It is a great way to be ready for the coming day.

CONTRIBUTORS

Liz Alcauskas and her husband Jim arrived in Woodbridge, Virginia, in September 1989. That same month they found the Bull Run Unitarian Universalists congregation while it was meeting at the Muriel Humphrey Center near their home. After their children Katie and Jacob left home to begin their adult lives and Liz and Jim retired from their FastSigns business, Liz began studying Spanish at Northern Virginia Community College in Woodbridge. Each spring, she enrolls in another Spanish class.

Ginny Ax, a native of Northern Virginia, graduated from Mary Washington College and did graduate work at the University of New Hampshire. She is married with one daughter, two stepsons, and five grandchildren. She was an elementary school teacher for thirty years. Her hobbies include freelance editing, decorating, antiquing, reading, traveling, and photography, for which she has won several awards. A member of Bull Run Unitarian Universalists congregation, she is a Fairfax County elections officer and is active in the Clifton Community Women's Club.

Lydia Bratton is a mixed media artist and art educator. She studied art at Northern Virginia Community College and Marymount University in Arlington, Virginia.

Davis Chung has happily wandered through life with the eye of a photographer and the heart of a writer. He takes note of the out-of-place, the majestic, and the truly odd. In 2010, Davis self-published his first book *Observations* in the Amazon Kindle format. He has published essays online and in a northern Maine journal. He lives in Manassas with the love of his life, Susan, and their two cats.

Steve Clapp served as a Peace Corps volunteer in Nigeria in the early Sixties. He then moved to Washington to evaluate antipoverty programs in the Midwest and Deep South as an inspector for the ill-fated U.S. Office of Economic Opportunity. He is now senior editor of *Food Chemical News*, a weekly newsmagazine specializing in food policy. He and his wife Bette Hileman keep busy with their blended family of five children and nine grandchildren.

Lori Connolly is a stay-at-home wife with cats and now a new puppy. Her family lives happily in Prince William County. She is a member of Bull Run Unitarian Universalists congregation.

Carol Covin is the author of *Who Gets to Name Grandma? The Wisdom of Mothers and Grandmothers* (© 2009 Twenty

Minutes Press). The book is based on forty interviews, half with mothers, half with grandmothers, in which Carol asks the question, "What are you not saying to each other?" Carol is a member of Bull Run Unitarian Universalists and a resident of Prince William County.

Michael J. Crowley began composing poetry in high school. For many years he wrote fitfully; then, in the early Nineties, he discovered open-mike poetry readings. Since then, he has participated in literally hundreds of readings. He has written poetry inspired by art works and jazz, and has read his work at fundraisers. He also led a poetry special-interest group associated with the Naturist Society.

Richard Demaret, a retired systems technician, considers himself Introverted Intuitive Feeling Perceiving as described in the Meyers-Briggs personality inventory. After growing up in Northern Virginia in the Fifties, he earned a business degree from Strayer University and held a number of electronics technician jobs. He is interested in business, economics, finance, world affairs, and writing. He has also given a great deal of thought to spiritual and philosophical issues.

Katherine Mercurio Gotthardt is a poetry and prose writer residing in western Prince William County, Virginia, where she enjoys exploring history, art, culture, and nature with her husband and children. An advocate for preservation, conservation, and civic engagement, Katherine volunteers for several non-profit organizations. She is a community writer for the regional newspaper *News & Messenger*, teaches college English composition online, and assists with teaching and assessing adult English language skills. Katherine facilitates the Writers' Group at Bull Run Unitarian Universalists. Her first book, *Poems from the Battlefield*, was released in 2009. Her children's book, illustrated by Selina Farmer, is forthcoming in 2011.

Bette Hileman is an independent writer and editor. She retired in 2008 from a twenty-seven-year career as a journalist at *Chemical & Engineering News*, the weekly newsmagazine of the American Chemical Society. Currently, she is working on poetry and a novel and has exhibited photos in several venues. She co-edited *Images in Ink*, an anthology that was published in 2010 by Windmore Foundation for the Arts, Culpeper, Virginia. Because of her pioneering articles covering climate change and the effects of toxic chemicals on health and the environment, she is listed in *Who's Who in the World* and *Who's Who in America*.

Ron Kendrick is a lifelong student of science and philosophy and a developer and early adopter of emerging technologies. He has survived near-death experiences that have expanded his perception of life and death. Ron and his wife have traveled the world for business and pleasure. He lives in Manassas, Virginia, and enjoys spending as much time as he can with his family.

Coleen Kivlahan, mother of two amazing sons Kevin and Nate, is a family physician and life-partner to Dave Higginbotham. Her career involves developing health policy for the Medicaid program in multiple states, providing medical care to uninsured populations, and performing political asylum examinations on victims of torture. Her personal life includes being outdoors as much as possible and laughing every chance she gets, as well as knitting, cooking, exercise, travel, and reading.

Rev. Nancy McDonald Ladd has served as minister to Bull Run Unitarian Universalists congregation since 2004. Before entering parish ministry, she studied theology at Xavier University and divinity at Meadville Lombard Theological School. She wrote a chapter for *Reverend X: How Generation X Ministers are Shaping Unitarian Universalism,* published by Jenkin Lloyd Jones Press, and a chapter for *A People So Bold: Theology and Ministry for Unitarian Universalists*, published by Skinner House Books. She also has contributed articles to *UU World.* She lives with her family in Centreville, Virginia.

Pat Malarkey is kept by Gem and Han Solo, two long-haired cats. As long as she works as a computer programmer to pay the mortgage and stock the pantry with cat food, her cats allow her to figure skate and ski. Gem and Han Solo *don't* know she's also a seminary student who is plotting to relocate them to California in 2012, where she will finish school. She will now erase her hard drive to keep the cats from learning about their impending move.

Alexandra Mooney, a sixth grader at Gainesville Middle School, loves animals, horseback riding, and the natural world. She eventually wants to become an "animal cop" to help protect animals. Alexandra attends the Bull Run Unitarian Universalists church, where she takes part in religious education and other activities.

Erika Mooney is an eighth grader at PACE West School in Haymarket, Virginia. An avid reader and a big fan of technology, she enjoys horseback riding and computer games. Erika attends Bull Run Unitarian Universalists church, where she takes part in religious education and other activities.

Jimmy Porter is a retired computer programmer. He served in the Army during the Vietnam War and later attended college in California. He has two children and two grandchildren. He is married to his soul mate Lola and is still trying to find himself.

Bruce Roemmelt lives on Bull Run Mountain with his beloved Beth. A retired firefighter from Prince William County, he's active in his firefighters union, the Virginia AFL/CIO, local politics, and in various capacities for Bull Run Unitarian Universalists congregation. Bruce served in the military from 1966 to 1970 and was stationed in Vietnam in 1968. He earned degrees from several colleges and universities, but still depends on Beth for editing and counsel.

Wanda Bryant Ruffin grew up in southern Alabama. She earned a B.A. in psychology and social studies at Huntingdon College, an M.A. in speech pathology and audiology from Auburn University, and degrees in counseling, human development, and nursing from Troy University. In 1964, she married James T. Ruffin and has a daughter Wende. She is retired from positions as speech pathologist and counselor at the Hospice of Montgomery County, and as founder and volunteer director of the Friends of Vietnam Veterans Memorial Project. Currently, she is enjoying her three granddaughters, managing rental properties, and studying Spanish.

Kathy Sanchez, a wife and mother, is a member of the Bull Run Unitarian Universalists congregation There, she is active in the Andean Spirituality Group, which meets for spiritual renewal, to foster a sense of community, and to practice healing on the three planes: physical, mental/emotional, and spiritual, following the Incan tradition and cosmology.

Sheila School is a retired music and special education teacher who lives with her dog Lilly in Lake Ridge, Virginia.

She is an active member of Bull Run Unitarian Universalists congregation and its writers group. She also serves on the board of directors of the Prince William League of Women Voters. She loves having time to pursue one of her favorite pastimes—writing.

Susan Sinclair was born June 4, 1940. Her parents, more captivated with a world careening toward war than with Susan, always referred to her as their "Dunkirk Babe." Seventy years and many wars later, she is trying to make sense of her long journey in this world by writing her memoirs. When inevitable questions of Truth arise, she generally strives for it, unless, like her father, she finds the opposite more fun.

Lily Stejskal, a recent graduate of Mary Baldwin College, hopes to become an author of children's books. She is a Pantheist and loves to write about Nature for any age group.

Christine Sunda lives with her husband, daughter, dog, and six cats in Centreville, Virginia. She loves hiking, traveling, canoeing, and gardening.

Larry S. Underwood taught biology at the Northern Virginia Community College. Before that, he held teaching and research positions at the University of Alaska, the University of Connecticut, and George Mason University. While in Alaska for twenty-five years, he became an expert in cold-tolerant mammals and refined a lifelong interest in environmental conservation. He has published several non-fiction books, including *BioInquiry*, a college-level, introductory biology textbook. Larry lives in Manassas, where he enjoys birding, political activism, spiritual growth, and keeping his wife Sally happy.

Sexton Music Studio

Christopher Sexton

Teaching Violin, Bluegrass Fiddle, Viola, Cello

9350 Main Street, Suite 309
Manassas, VA 20110
(in the Bull Run Unitarian Universalist Church Building)

Phone: (703) 975-5075
christopher.sexton@comcast.net
http://www.sextonmusicstudio.com

EDITING AND PHOTOGRAPHY

BETTE HILEMAN

17267 Banbury Court
Jeffersonton, Virginia 22724
703-677-2828

bette.hileman@gmail.com

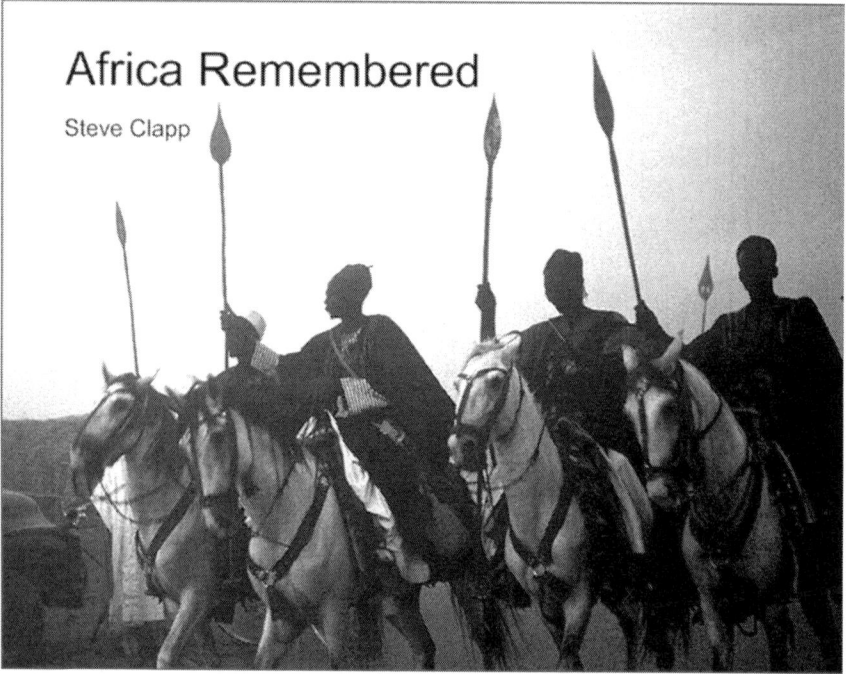

Africa Remembered

Steve Clapp

Africa Remembered: Adventures in Post-Colonial Nigeria and Beyond is a lavishly-illustrated coffee-table book based on letters home and color slides. BRUU author Steve Clapp, an early Peace Corps volunteer, taught in a secondary boarding school, trekked across the remote Mambila Plateau, and traveled home through politically turbulent Central and East Africa.

"Steve Clapp had a Peace Corps experience worth writing home about— and he did. He uses a narrative style that makes his Peace Corps experience accessible to former volunteers and non-volunteers alike. His story is well-written and beautifully photographed, and I strongly recommend it." —Bryant Wieneke, Peace Corps Worldwide

"This is a beautifully designed paperback with sumptuous photography. Africa Remembered *is a fascinating read, covering aspects of the African experience seldom mentioned in Peace Corps memoirs."*—David Strain, Friends of Nigeria

Africa Remembered is available through Amazon and in the gift shop of the Smithsonian Museum of African Art. You can buy it at cost from the author by e-mailing scclapp@gmail.com

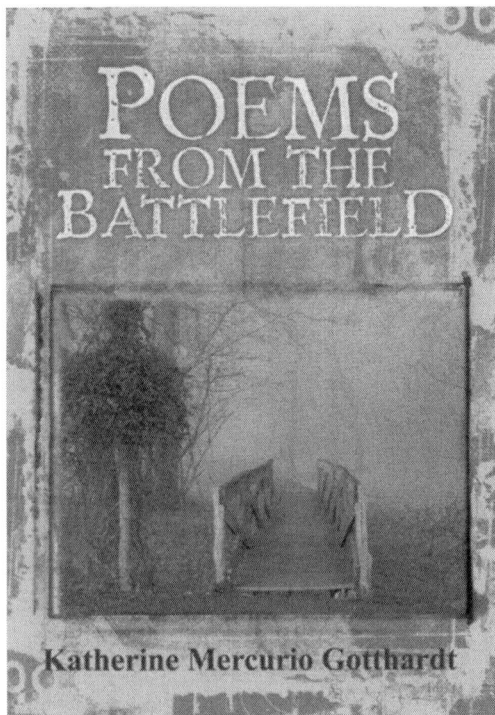

POEMS
FROM THE
BATTLEFIELD

Katherine Mercurio Gotthardt

Original, contemporary poetry based on the Civil War, original and archival photos, and period quotes take readers on an exceptional trip through history.

"...visually haunting, with sepia-toned pages and black & white photos—some of them shot in modern time—frozen in the 150-year past."
–Cindy Brookshire, Author & 2010 Manassas Woman of the Year

"Like some of the world's greatest poets who changed actions or the course of governments by portraying the human suffering of nations and individuals, Gotthardt, through her book of poems, takes us to our deepest empathy for the people and natural surroundings that were sacrificed by war."
–George Layne, Founder, Gainesville-Haymarket Rotary

"Few poetry collections to date can compare."
–Clinton Foster, Author

A portion of the proceeds from this book is donated to support historic preservation efforts.
www.PoemsfromtheBattlefield.com

LEAGUE OF WOMEN VOTERS®

WANTED: New members

FOR WHAT: A nationally known, old, highly respected service and educational association.

HOURS: It's up to you.

REQUIRED SKILLS: Curiosity and a desire to help others.

OTHER REQUIREMENTS: Citizen of U.S., at least 18 years of age. Both men and women are welcome.

COST: Reasonable.

CONTACT: Sheila School at shesh1957@gmail.com.

7676390R0

Made in the USA
Charleston, SC
30 March 2011